W9-CEZ-631

Rivertown Risk

Rivertown Risk

JOE L. HENSLEY

PUBLISHED FOR THE CRIME CLUB BY

DOUBLEDAY & COMPANY, INC.

GARDEN CITY, NEW YORK

1977

All of the characters in this book
are fictitious, and any resemblance
to actual persons, living or dead,
is purely coincidental.

ISBN: 0-385-11224-6
Library of Congress Catalog Card Number 75-38164
Copyright © 1977 by Joe L. Hensley
All Rights Reserved
Printed in the United States of America
First Edition

1

Courthouse

That morning, before we began jury selection again, Deputy Sheriff Joe Pierceton showed me the scratches on the door to Ed's probation office. The door was heavy, one of those metal doors they started making a few years back when public disorders began to make courthouses more hazardous.

There were unmistakable signs of tampering near the lock: scratches, signs of hammering.

Pierceton nodded at the door. "You got you a prowler," he said.

"Did whoever it was get in?" I asked.

"Not through that door. You can get through one of them, but it's work. Could be something scared him off." He nodded to himself, eyes shining. "Maybe he'll come back. Would it be okay if I slept over here for a few nights?"

"You want to, Joe?"

"Sure. I'll get my sleeping bag, Judge."

"Sheriff won't like it."

"He won't even know. I'm off duty. I've got one of those radio pagers that I keep at hand. It'll beep at me if they try to reach me at home."

"I really think . . ."

"Someone killed Ed and now someone is trying to get into his office," Joe said stolidly. "I'll need to borrow a key."

I had an extra. I got it off the chain and gave it to him. It had once been Ed's key. "This is a master," I said.

"What if you need to get in?"

"I've got another key." I shook my head. "Sheriff catches you up here helping me and he'll make it mean on you, Joe."

He shook his head. He had a good smile. I thought he was perhaps four or five years younger than me.

"He's sure working hard for Mr. Bobbin," he said. "Him and Mr. Walker have people in every night sitting around that big table back in the kitchen. They drink coffee and cuss you and try to figure out every vote in the organization." He shook his head ruefully. "If they wasn't so hard about it I think they'd do better. People don't like to be told. But they'll be buyin' votes against you on Primary Day. And they'll have the troops out. They'll be voting the cemeteries and the nursing homes." He shook his head again. "They are out to get your rear end, Judge." He laughed without looking at me.

Later, we adjourned for the day at about three o'clock when we reached a convenient point. Prosecuting Attorney Allen Dunwich had just again passed the jury to George Higer. It was the fourth day of *voir dire* examination of jurors and it had been cut and slash conflict all the way. Higer, from the metropolis across the river, was trying hard to live up to his reputation of being a strutting rooster of a trial lawyer and Dunwich, never one to shy from a fight, was enjoying mixing it up with him.

They both followed me into my tiny office and together we admired the cracks in my walls and the grimy windows the janitors still chose to ignore. Outside a thin, spring rain fell and farmers crowded around the doors of the courthouse waiting for plowing weather.

"How much longer do you gentlemen estimate this will take?" I asked.

"I don't know, Judge," Higer said fretfully. He adjusted his tie a fraction. He was fiftyish. One got the impression that his face was half eyebrows. Despite the rigors of the day he still looked as if he'd just stepped out of an exclusive clothier's. "Perhaps another week."

Dunwich grinned. "I'm ready when he is, Your Honor."

Privately I didn't believe it would take very much longer than perhaps the first of the week. Both sides were down to two remaining peremptory challenges, the only means by which they could remove an unfriendly juror without cause. You get careful at that stage. You try to get rid of fanatics by challenges for cause rather than using the precious peremptories because a fanatic will always find some way of relating his cause area to the case he's trying. There is no way of knowing which way he/she will go. And the size of the fanatic herd seems to grow from year to year—religious nuts, non-religious nuts, anti-communists, far right, far left, null tax, welfare state, etc., etc.

I said: "We'll work in the morning, but I plan to adjourn tomorrow afternoon for the funeral of my bailiff."

Both of them nodded.

One of Higer's several aides came to the open door. He tiptoed in and whispered in Higer's ear.

"May I be excused, Judge Tostini?" Higer asked. "Duty calls."

"Of course."

Higer removed himself to the hall. Out there I could see him conferring with his client, Amos Walker. The two extra bailiffs I'd hired guarded my door and watched Higer and Amos curiously. I could tell that Amos was upset about something, but then he was normally upset just now. Deputy Sheriff Joe Pierceton, Amos's sometime guard and my confidant in the sheriff's office, had moved politely out of earshot and was waiting unobtrusively.

Dunwich could also see the hall scene. He sat in his chair, covertly watching and enjoying. He belongs to that other party, normally heavy losers in my county, but he'd been elected when my own party tried hard to re-elect a bumptious clown prosecutor to a third term two years back.

He said in a low voice: "I don't know whether I'm going to get the job done here or not, Judge, but Amos deserves to have it happen to him. Long, long overdue. You wonder how someone who's killed another person can still stay like Amos is, full of venom, ready to snap at the world."

"One who kills makes his own excuses, Al. Somehow,

inside himself, he makes it right that he did what he did or he builds himself a fantasy that it was done by someone else."

He smiled and nodded philosophically and stretched. "How about a quick Beefeater's?"

"Thanks, Al. Pass for tonight."

He smiled again vaguely and got up and wandered on out. He's a very good prosecutor, soft-voiced, effective. He's been hell on the local drug trade, and on thieves and big-time gamblers, mean as Drāno, uncompromising. He's mid-thirtyish, a handsome man with slightly too much chin and too little nose for some, according to Jen, my court stenographer. He likes his job. If he has a fault, it's that he's become enamored of being prosecutor and lately has taken each case personally, working up an individual hate for each defendant. And he drinks too much these days. It isn't serious yet, but it's going in that direction. I like him. He's as honest and thorough and fair as a man can be in his difficult job. I also like his wife, Ellie.

Amos Walker and George Higer still conferred in the hall. Amos had been indicted for first degree murder, accused of beating his young wife, Janet's, head in with some sort of never found blunt instrument. I remembered that wife well from political functions. She'd been much younger than Amos, a lady with a Bourbon breath and available eyes, acres of figure, in and out, up and down. A whistle stop. Amos had publicly threatened her for her miscues a number of times. I probably shared the vague idea of the town that he'd married her to war on time, to combat the condition of growing old. Some think they can do that. They take their pills, have their faces lifted by cunning surgeons, wear hair pieces, and make themselves finally younger by discarding the old wife and taking a new model. They never worry about what will happen after.

For Amos all had been turmoil *after*.

She'd been killed in their house as she'd apparently been packing to leave him for perhaps the tenth time. Amos had been seen around the house near the time of death. He had no alibi. There'd been overheard sounds of a fight. One of his jackets, later found concealed in the basement, had bloodstains like hers on it. The telephone had been torn from the wall.

Despite a massive hunt the murder weapon had never been found.

Plenty of evidence to move to trial. Enough to hold him without bond. Let a jury decide.

Amos had been a big part of my life once. I was sorry for him now. And he hated me.

I shrugged and went at some paper work which had stacked up, signing routine matters. When I looked up again it was after four and the hall outside was empty. Jen had vanished early and I remembered she'd said she had some other business to attend to before going to the funeral home. I could still smell her subtle perfume.

I locked the office, for what good it would do. The janitors had keys. I'd found files messed up, drawers opened and searched, crushed cigarettes in the ash trays. So I carried anything I didn't want seen in my head.

Down the long hall things were still moving in superior court, which takes up the other half of the third floor. As I stepped past, Judge Arnold "Arnie" File came out of his

courtroom. We smiled cordially at each other, but it isn't
that way at all between us—now. He's fifteen years older
than me, a big gray man gone heavily to paunch. When I
first was appointed to the bench he helped me a lot. But
now friendship has cooled. Once, years back, Judge File
was county chairman for our party. A man like Amos
holding the chairman's position was automatically close to
Judge Arnie. Too many years of politics had made the
man carefully sly. Now it was hard for him to make direct
confrontations, take stands which were unhealthy, un-
popular.

He was accompanied by lawyers and his court stenographer and bailiff. I heard them all laughing together as
they stood there. A dirty joke? A golf story? I envied him
his easy ability with people.

He saw me and waved his companions away genteelly.
"Come inside, Mickey. I need to talk to you."

"All right, Judge," I said. I've always been "Mickey" to
him and he's always been "Judge" to me. A pecking order
perhaps.

His crowd of retainers eyed me curiously and then
melted away.

His office was the same size mine was, but similarity
ended there. When Amos and I had fallen out, the janitorial people stopped taking more than cursory care of my
end of the third floor. For a time they'd not even bothered
to empty the wastebaskets, but that had stopped when
someone had dumped them at the superior court end of
the hall one night. I didn't know who'd done it and
planned no investigation. After that, simple things got
done, but my offices were still bleak and dirty. Somehow

the heat ceased to work right. It was always too hot or too cold. The windows were filmed with dirt, the carpet discolored and in need of sweeping. In Judge File's rooms all was warm, well kept, almost cozy. But then the janitors were hired by the party—a fact of life.

We sat.

"I don't keep booze in here or I'd offer you a drink," he said lightly.

I nodded and waited. Sooner or later he'd get to it.

"I'm going to have to do something I don't want much to do, Mickey," he said solemnly, looking away from me.

"How's that, Judge," I said, knowing.

"I'm going to have to back your primary opponent."

I smiled. "Thanks for telling me."

"I try to be honest and open."

I kept from laughing. It had been Arnie who'd come to see me when three of the medium-high druggies had been jury convicted in my court, who'd talked about suspended sentences, who'd asked a dozen oblique questions about "how much."

"Is that what you wanted to tell me?" I asked.

He nodded and watched me curiously. Maybe he expected me to plead with him, try to change his mind.

I got up and we nodded again at each other. I went on out and left him to his paper shuffling.

I elevatored down to the first floor of the courthouse. Most everything was now closed, but the Recorder's Office was still open and the recorder sat in the middle of his office in the big, wingback chair he affected, the one wags liked to refer to as his "throne."

He nodded amiably to me.

"Hi, Judge," he said. He spat an amber stream of tobacco juice into his private spittoon and offered me a bite from a dusty plug he extracted from a pocket.

"Good stuff," he encouraged.

"No, thanks," I said carefully.

His name is Gosport McFay and he's been in office in our courthouse since I can remember. He knows the town and loves it and puts up with the foibles of its citizenry. He's served ably at every job he's won. Now he's getting along in years and those long years have gaunted him down to brown hide and raw bones and not much else. He stays in office because he's smart and honest and because he politicks, in his own way, 365 days a year. His politicking way is pretty unique and hard to believe. He *helps* anyone who comes through his door if that person can be helped. *Crazy.* Certainly not the American tradition.

"You want to go to the funeral home with me?" I asked.

He shook his head stolidly. "I went down for a bit this morning. A bad place. As old as I'm getting it hardly seemed worth the time to leave, so now I ain't going back until the funeral."

He and my deceased bailiff had been close friends.

"What would Ed have been doing in that neighborhood where he was hit and killed?"

Gosport's old eyes flickered. I'm never sure of him when I ask him a question allowing him to guess at an answer. He knows as much as any man about what goes on in my town, so much that he hates ever to admit to a lack of knowledge. And so there must be an answer.

He said in his thin voice: "That's a very bad section of town as both of us know. Almost as bad as living across the bridge." He cackled and nodded in the direction of our neighbor metropolis across the river. "I'd bet that Ed was checking things. Maybe for the sheriff. Ed never had figured out he was supposed to be retired from that kind of thing."

"And a hit-run driver got him? Accident?" I asked, unconvinced.

"Maybe," he said stolidly. "He wasn't real quick on his feet any more. Lots of hot-rodders out there. Lots of mean bastards too. Welfare cheaters. Maybe someone with a grudge against him just happened to see Ed, then ambushed him, ran him down a-purpose."

There was the Hickory Hill section of town. Once it had been block after block of neat, cracker-box houses built by subdividers for buyers with G.I. money. That was about thirty years back and now the neighborhood was run-down houses on tiny lots, sagging, gutterless roofs, gravel drives and boarded-up windows. It was a refuge for those defeated by my town and the city across the river, but not a safe refuge. Bill collectors still cautiously prowled the neighborhood in numbers and police cars patrolled it heavily, at least during the day.

"Sheriff say anything to you about Ed checking something for him, Gosport?" I asked, fighting down an upsurge of guilt I'd reasoned away until now. If Ed hadn't been doing something for the sheriff he could have been doing something for me. Politicking.

"Me'n the sheriff, we don't talk a whole bunch these days. He thinks I've got the knife out for him. I ain't real bad yet, but it's getting to be a temptation. When he gets the way he is I just let him be a temptation. When he gets wanting to perform what he does best and that's kiss at me about halfway down my backside." He smiled and it was like a crack appearing in a statue. "Ed did things because he thought they needed doing, not because of Sheriff Zisk and his help. Only thing sheriff's deputies is real good for these days is knocking kids' heads."

"All right," I said.

"How goes it upstairs?" he asked, lowering his voice some.

"Still picking a jury."

"Bad news in that one, Mickey," he said, lecturing me a little. "Amos is holding what's happened against people." His look let me know I was one of the chief unfortunates Amos Walker would soon punish.

"He could have removed me from the bench," I said. "A change of venue was automatic at one time. All he had to do was file for it."

"That ain't Amos's way. He's been running party things around here for a lot of years. Just because he supposedly knocked his wife's head in don't change nothing about that. People who get out in front of him and make him slow up are going to get hurt. Not only that, but I guess he's figured by now you've helped make him a dead dog if he tries to run for state office. He got mad at Ed and beat him for sheriff a few years back. He gets convicted of less than first degree and he'll get out on bond and appeal it to death. He's got friends up in the capital, high friends. But that don't mean that someone ain't going to have to pay and take the blame for all the trouble he's got into." He nodded. "That's you. You didn't give him bond originally. You kept him in jail. You humbled him."

Gosport was right. Amos had been running my party and this end of the state for a lot of years. He hadn't liked it when I signed his political enemy, the now deceased Ed Long, on as my bailiff and, again, when I employed Jen. Maybe he'd felt I owed him something for those transgressions. He'd left me on the bench. And, after a long hearing, I hadn't admitted him to bond. But I'd never promised him anything for the judgeship. He'd sought me out and asked me to take it. I'd accepted it only after I'd been promised a free hand.

"Who's the only candidate for a major office, except maybe the sheriff, who has significant primary opposition?" Gosport asked solemnly.

"I guess that's me," I said. "I know he's hot after me, Gosport."

"Primary won't draw flies," he continued mercilessly. "Walker tells the organization to dump you and most of them will dump you. You take forty plus precincts with maybe thirty people in each one who can be fingered and you're going to get beat blue probably. I know. I've seen it happen."

"You mean to Ed?"

"Ed and others."

"You've beaten Amos," I said. "I've heard around that

he doesn't have any use for you, but you keep getting nominated and elected."

He leaned toward me. "That's 'cause I know where a lot of skeletons is buried. That's 'cause a lot of folks owe me. Amos can scream about me all he wants, but as long as I can get out and see my people he's going to have one hell of a time laying me out." He nodded, almost to himself. "He tells them precinct people one thing about me, but I tell them another, Judge Mickey. But that don't mean you can do the same thing I do."

"All right."

He shook his head. "No, it ain't all right." He examined me. "I'm going to go under the notion you want to be elected judge. I mean you took the appointment when Judge Olson died."

"I'm a candidate," I said.

"Well I want you to know that you ain't got a very big chance because I know the word's out not to back you."

"Judge File just told me upstairs that he's going to back my opponent, Perry Bobbin."

That stopped him a little. He didn't like Judge File much.

I thought about it while he was short of words. I'd thought about it before. I did want to be elected. I liked the job of being circuit court judge and thought I'd been fairly competent at it. But there was nothing I could do to lessen Amos's anger at me. I was a mere functionary in a situation which would go its inexorable way toward an unforeseeable end. And for me to tamper with it in any fashion at all would make my life useless to me.

"You can maybe help yourself some," Gosport said, sof-

tening a little. "Smile more at folks on the street. Take
more time with them. Some are saying your family arrived here from Italy with nothing but a banana cart and
a spade half a century back and now you're Circuit Judge
Michael Tostini and it's made you uppity."

"I'll work at being friendly," I said. "I'll kiss babies.
Eighteen years and up."

"You do that," he said grinning. "I know you ain't a bit
uppity, Mickey. But the average citizen of this town
don't know you well enough to decide that. All he
knows is what he hears and sees. Amos knows how to win
a primary. He's won a lot of them. He'll look for every
place he can gouge you, knee you. You can bet he'll try
the uppity bit." He nodded. "Wear that arm you've got
with the hook on it for a while—so that the town can see
again you're a wounded veteran. You can put it away and
wear that nice-looking one you've got on now after the
primary."

"Should I wear my lapel ribbon, too?" I asked.

"Don't be sarcastic with me, Mickey. Sure you should
wear it. Ain't very many people around here ever got the
Navy Cross. It helped you get the appointment to fill out
for Judge Olson and it can help you again."

"Thanks, Gosport," I said. But I knew I wouldn't wear
the hooklike arm. Not any more. No more self-pity even
by allowing myself symbols of it. Not even if it cost me
the election. The ribbon was different. It stood for something else. But the hook arm brought back those days
when I was less than a whole man, when I'd admitted it
to myself, given in to it. I wasn't even sure I knew where

it was and then, having opened the door, I remembered. It was in my closet upstairs in the office.

"You go on now," he said. "If you want to know anything from the sheriff, you'd best ask him. Then tell me what he says. But don't tell him you're going to pass on anything to me."

"All right," I said, smiling. I'd been taking orders and getting advice from Gosport for a lot of years. The fact of me being judge hadn't changed things.

He slid his big chair toward a desk and began to shuffle papers, pointedly ignoring me. My audience for the day was over.

I went out into the coolness. Late April rain was still falling and the sky was gray with still more of it. Pigeons fluttered about the courthouse roof, crowding against each other when they alighted, seeking a dry spot, warmth.

The courthouse wall, normally crowded, was almost vacant because of the weather.

I started toward the sheriff's office in the next building by way of the courthouse complex, but saw his parking space was vacant.

There would be time enough later. He'd be at the funeral, maybe at the funeral home. I wanted to get to that funeral home. But first a shower.

2

Home Place

Home for me was a big house which my father lovingly rebuilt thirty-plus years back. Three stories of what had once been Gothic elegance and now was dowdy, old lady. It needed paint. It always needed paint. It was a hodge-podge of dripping porches, pillars, gingerbread, and high windows. Pop had scrimped and saved and bought it when he had visions of a large family. I was the firstborn. High expectations. A long time later there'd been my sister. That was all.

I'd grown up in the house, played football down the street, swung in the big trees, and cut the grass and raked leaves all of my young years, for Pop had not believed in a boy not working and not playing.

He'd died when I was in 'Nam and left the house as his legacy, to Mom and me and my sister. He'd died in one of the familiar, unpleasant ways we accept for ourselves—a car accident which had also left mother paralyzed from the waist down. Eight years back now. When I was discharged I'd come back and entered practice in the town, joined the veterans' organizations, which collectively distrusted 'Nam veterans (I mean after all didn't we *lose* that war?), and tried to make enough money for us to live. Somehow I'd kept us above water, but the good cases, the big money cases, went to other lawyers, other law firms. For a while I'd blamed it on the fact that I was missing part of an arm. It was easier that way. I'd edged around the sides of the arena, fighting misdemeanors in city court, trying divorces for the almost indigent, writing contracts and deeds. Rivertown had a lot of lawyers. I was one of them; no more, no less than others, except when I sought excuses.

The appointment as judge of the circuit court had been an answer. The money was considerably more than had been coming in. Things still weren't loose and easy, but now we paid our bills as they came due and most of the old ones were paid in full. Downtown merchants smiled at me amiably.

I went in and wiped my feet on a rug at the door. Mom was out on the enclosed sun porch. She sat in her wheel chair inspecting the wet world outside. The sun porch was her favorite place even when there was no sun to warm it. She kept the room full of potted plants and flowers, puttering with them constantly, petting them, loving them.

All the first floor of the house was her domain. Now and then, when she became overrestless, we'd take her up to the second and third floors of the house and let her see we weren't living in filth, let her lovingly clean. But the first floor was hers and she kept it sterile as an operating table, cooked our meals there, and lived as regent of her own small, insulated world.

She smiled at me and turned her cheek up for a routine kiss.

"Hello, son."

"Where's sis?" I asked, when first greetings were done. She shrugged eloquently. "Still at school probably. And I think she may have had a sorority meeting. She said she might be late." She nodded, sorting out the day and its requirements. "Are you going to drive me to the funeral home?"

"After I grab a shower and change clothes."

"Bad day?"

I shook my head, refusing to admit it had been. "Trial in progress is all."

"Amos Walker. Years ago I used to know him and his first wife. An arrogant man. Your father had no use for him."

I examined her. Except for the wheel chair she looked very good. Her face seemed younger than her fifty-three years and her body wasn't wasted below the point where movement ceased. Therapists came three times a week and worked with her. She was bright and amiable, interested and undefeated. The accident which had killed Pop and crippled her was a thing she'd abandoned back someplace in her past. She'd accepted it and walled around it. She hadn't let it make her less than she was, except in subtle ways. It had made her so she believed in only the world she saw around her, so that answers were too simple for her. Because of the continual lack of money she constantly involved herself in projects intended to move her upward and make her self-supporting. She'd learned to run an electric typewriter competently and she typed papers for college kids and sometimes took jobs as a home addresser. Once, worried because the phone kept answering busy, I drove home to find her busily working as a telephone canvaser for some encyclopedia sales outfit.

The cross she now bore was that nothing she did ever brought in much money. She could sit there on her sun porch and count to the penny what was spent each month, then weigh that amount against what she could bring in, and the two figures were vastly different.

Even if I now did favorably balance that money situation, I was, in a way, another defeat. She dreamed constantly of grandchildren and there I was, thirty-three years old, not yet married, worse—not even planning marriage. If she could make enough money, then maybe I would marry. That was one of her major dreams. All my protests availed me little. She knew I was dating Jenny Green, my court reporter. That was enough, as it had been with past girls she'd approved of, for her to move from A to Z and again plan my future, married life. She was incurable that way.

She was happy only in the local world around her that she so intimately knew. Twice, over her semi-objections, I'd bundled her into the car and taken her to Florida for a week or so. Not even the sight of my sister knocking them dead on the beach had pleased her. She'd ignored the warm weather, ignored the sea, and not been happy until we were home again.

Now, she wheeled over to a table and flecked an invisible speck of dust from the gleaming surface.

"You go on and shower then," she ordered. "I'll be ready."

I nodded and went up the stairs. I undressed and removed my artificial hand. It consisted of a plastic shell that fitted over my arm below the elbow stub. The shell had a metal wrist joint, covered, and was then attached to a very natural-looking hand. There's a light shoulder harness and a cable runs down from it cunningly to the hand. I can shrug my shoulders and tighten the hand, but it really doesn't work well enough to do complicated things with it.

I took a shower and shaved and examined myself in the mirror. There I was, Michael Tostini. I wasn't overly impressed with what I saw. The only thing that was different about me was the left arm, gone ten inches below the elbow. There was some heavy scarring at chest level, scars that puckered and hurt sometimes in cold weather, just as the missing hand still hurt. And so, I was a little less, rather than more.

I remembered what Gosport had said about the hook and that it was in the closet in my office. I doubted the janitors would bother it. It isn't really a hook, but it sort of looks like one. It's a device which can be made to open and close by the same type of shoulder webbing and manipulation as the hand, except it works better. I used to wear it and get some mileage out of it—pity, shock, even a little fear.

I put my artificial hand back on. It looks pretty real, but as I said it really doesn't function very well. A doctor at the V.A. hospital told me that, if I wanted to try, they could hook up a device to my biceps muscle by means of surgery and that might work very well. I hadn't tried it and didn't think I ever would try it. It made me hurt inside just thinking about it.

When I got downstairs Mom looked me over critically. "You look better," she said.

She'd put on a colorful jacket she likes and she was ready to go.

"Thank you," I said. "So do you."

I rolled her down the incline we had put next to the steps, lifted her into the front, turn-out seat that Chevrolet has put into its Monte Carlos, then folded her wheel chair and put it into the back seat. We were ready.

As was her habit she reached over, turned on the radio to the local station and caught a twangy-voiced announcer in the midst of an ad that extolled the virtues of my primary opponent. She snapped the radio off.

"It'll be over soon."

She nodded grimly. "Win or lose?" she asked.

"Yes."

"Why don't you buy some radio advertising? Some newspaper ads?"

"They cost a lot of money, Mom. And people don't believe that sort of thing anyway."

"We can spare the money."

"No. No radio ads—no newspaper ads. Ed went that route, Mom. Amos Walker controls the newspaper and the radio station. When Ed tried, somehow his ads got fouled up. I'm not going to pay someone to sabotage me."

We drove sedately through my town to the funeral

home. There was a crowd of cars parked outside, but I spotted a car leaving near the entrance and parked in the vacated spot. I got Mom back into her folding wheel chair smoothly and we went inside.

Jenny Green, my court reporter, met us at the door and I smiled and looked her over. There's a lot to see. I'm an inch over six feet. With low heels on she looks me squarely in the eyes. She's built in proportion to her height, a large lovely woman with alive, glossy brown hair and eyes that are sometimes blue, sometimes green, sometimes almost gray. She's a solemn girl and her smiles are sudden and worth waiting for. She has the high attraction that some tall women seem to own. She can turn heads sideways in church; she can turn angry visiting lawyers and judges into lambs. And yet her face isn't really beautiful. Perhaps it's something more than mere beauty. Her mouth is generous, her nose too small, her eyes a little wide, a lot larger than normal. When you put it all together with the body below, men get all slack-jawed and either overhesitant or overforward when they see her.

She is one of those rare people who worries about the state of the world and those inhabitants of it she comes into contact with. I've seen her eyes dim with tears for some unwanted, troubled juvenile. She has sympathy for anyone who *needs*. Still, she has a basic toughness wherein she can recognize the final line when further compromise will do no good.

She is a combination of moods. Her life has not been easy. Sometimes she can be butterfly gay. Sometimes she is somber and sad.

She is much woman.

Once, before she came to work for me, she worked for Amos Walker. Under present circumstances that has caused some ripples in the town, some snide stories. I doubt those stories benefit Amos Walker and probably, in the way of such stories, don't benefit Jen or me.

Now, she smiled shyly at Mom and took charge of the wheel chair. I spied Sheriff Zisk in a group of men off to the side of the big, adjoining parlor room and went that way.

"I'll join you ladies in the viewing room after a bit," I said.

I went on over to the group of men. I knew all of them in varying degrees. There were two minor office holders, one ward captain, a retired city policeman, and Sheriff Henry "Hen" Zisk, the current proprietor of the brisk trades conducted in the sheriff's office. In my town a sheriff seldom dies broke.

Hen's a thin, muscular man probably a little over fifty years old. I've never seen him out of uniform since his election and he was in it now, all shiny gold badges and shoulder insignia, silver name plate, plus squeaking leather belt, stiff creased pants booted in tight at the bottom. I wondered what he wore to bed.

He gave me a careful, election year smile.

"Hi, Judge," he said.

I nodded. Even before I fell out of favor with the party hierarchy we didn't like each other well. He's a competent cold craftsman at his job, far more interested in headlines and his coming re-election than in the people in trouble he deals with. And he's Amos Walker's man, body and soul, hand clutching billfold. As such he was holding meetings for Amos in his jail, erecting Perry Bobbin signs wherever available space could be found, publicly praising Perry and bad-mouthing me. He'd been rewarded for that sort of non-deviant conduct by no party-split backed candidate filing against him for sheriff. First time in years it had happened. He had only one opponent and that one, from what I heard, was a reformed drunk who'd come out without any party stalwart's help. So Zisk was pretty sure he'd be renominated and, if county politics followed their normal course, elected for four more years in the fall. He eyed me with the slight arrogance of the confident toward the unsure.

We'd not yet clashed openly. I thought he was being careful. I'd not allowed Amos Walker admitted to bond, but the sheriff was giving him a sort of bond on his own. I'd heard he even drove him places. I'd ignored it as the lesser of evils. It was his jail.

"See you in private a moment, Sheriff?" I asked.

He nodded without enthusiasm and we moved to a window while the survivors of his conversation group eyed us curiously. I figured within fifteen minutes some one of them would report to Amos Walker that we'd held a conversation together and that, within twenty minutes, Sheriff Hen Zisk would pass on every word of our conversation. That couldn't be helped.

"Was Ed looking into something particular for you?" I asked.

He smiled slightly and relaxed a little. When you work openly against a man politically you never know if you're going to get lashed for it. He hadn't been sure what it was I wanted. Now he knew.

"Wasn't doin' nothing for me, Judge," he said. He hesitated for a moment. I'd caught him off guard and the question was unexpected. "He was in maybe a week or so ago to see me, but I missed him. He told Joey Pierceton that he had some hot drug news and that he'd be back later to fill us in if anything come of it. But he never came back."

"You have any further information about what happened to him—how he died?"

"City people checked it, Judge. You'd have to ask them." He yawned for effect, his eyes not veiling his contempt for me. "All I heard was that it was some kind of hit-run."

"I see."

He'd given me enough. It was time to seek something in trade for it.

"How goes your trial?" he asked, voice lowered.

"All right. The lawyers are still working on trying to get a jury."

"From all I know the prosecutor ain't got a chance of getting Amos. Politics is all it is." He gave me his best confident look. "Be better for you that way. Take some of the heat off you." He nodded. "A smart man might even make a little political hay off that if it ain't too late. And it ain't too late, Mickey. I know. He's mad, but he's still reasonable."

"I never was smart, Hen. You know that. I'm just a poor bastard trying to do his job."

His face hardened a little, but the smile never left it. "Sure," he said, completely unconvinced that there wasn't a word somewhere which could fix all the problems and make Amos shiny again.

"I ate before I was judge," I said.

He backed one step away. "I know that. But you want to get elected judge, don't you?"

"Frankly, Hen," I lied without changing expression, "I don't give a damn."

His mouth worked a little. I'd taken Christmas away from him for a moment. Later I knew he'd work it out to come out his way. Everyone wants to be elected. They have to want it. It's the American Way.

I saw that realization come to him and he had one more word for me: "Old friend of yours broke out of prison last night."

"Oh?"

He couldn't wait. It was that good. "Chili Blackwell," he said, smiling.

I nodded. I remembered Chili very well. He was a half animal I'd inherited to try from my deceased predecessor on the bench. A jury had convicted him of rape. He'd threatened the jurors, threatened the witnesses, threatened the world. Mostly he'd threatened me.

"Watch yourself," he said, smiling hugely. I saw it had given him great pleasure to tell me. "Watch your family. You know how Chili is with women."

"Oh, you'll protect us, Hen," I said softly.

He didn't know exactly how to take that and so he nodded stoutly.

We parted company and I went into the viewing room, leaving him to report to his cronies his version of our conversation.

Jenny had pushed Mom up to a crowd of ladies and Mom was involved in earnest discussion with Ed's half sister and some other older ladies I didn't recognize. I nodded and smiled and Jen gave me a conspiratorial wink.

Ed lay trussed in a suit, in his final bed, eyes closed and tie neatly knotted for once. I hoped that wherever he was there was a good supply of Kentucky Bourbon and plenty of chewing tobacco. We'd been friends for a very long time and there was a huge empty space inside me, full of chunks of ice. I knew that spot would never completely vanish. Maybe it wasn't as large as when I'd lost Pop, but it was more recent and so more raw.

I stood there and looked at him and the room dimmed around me. He could be laying dead because he'd been seeking political support for my failing fortunes.

I turned morosely away. At the side of the room Mom was still involved in avid conversation with Ed's half sister and her other friends. Jen had joined in. They ignored me.

For some reason women have many mysterious things to talk about when they group together. Should a man move up to one of those conferences he's either ignored or the group becomes overpolite until he moves on.

Back in the corner of the room, staring out into the cold, rainy night, I saw Captain Tiny Quinn, who's in charge of the city detective bureau.

I went on over. We shook hands.

"How you running, Judge?" he asked. His nickname is a joke. He's a big man who is placid and steady and pretty bright. He's testified in my court on several occa-

sions and I like and respect him. He's also an old school-
mate of Amos Walker's and I've heard he's made some
statements about belief in Amos's innocence.

"Doesn't sound too bad or too good," I said. "I guess I
won't know until the votes are counted."

"You'll get most of the department votes," he said, and
I half believed him. "Enough and more to make up for
what that silly sheriff costs you. Way I hear it friend
Amos was most shook up because you stole his girl." He
nodded across the room, toward where Jen was.

"I did catch some hell when I hired her," I admitted.

"Lot of girl," he said. "Wish I was about twenty years
younger."

"She is that and I'm glad you're not."

He smiled and looked back out at the rain. It seemed to
be falling harder.

"I think they got the wrong man on Amos," he said.

"Could be. But a grand jury indicted him and now he's
on trial. If you've got evidence you ought to go see Mr.
Higer, Amos's attorney."

"Sure," he said.

"Did you check out Ed Long?" I asked, changing the
subject.

"Yes."

"Anything out of the way about that one?"

He looked at me and seemed to decide for me. He
moved a little closer and lowered his voice confidentially.
"It isn't for publication yet, Judge, but he wasn't killed
where we discovered the body."

I was startled. "I'd thought it was just a hit and run."

"It seemed that way at first. But there wasn't very

much blood. Not enough of it where we found him. Dead men don't bleed. So we think someone may have killed him elsewhere and then hauled him out there late and run over him with a car, probably a stolen one. My bet is that the subject vehicle is across the river now, burned or buried. They can afford it."

"Who can afford it?"

"The drug bunch. Ed was very bad medicine to them. He had lots of young punk friends. Ed was good with kids, maybe the best I've ever seen. They talked to him, liked him, and he liked them. It was a two-way street. Now and then he'd pass something on to us, but never so a kid got hurt. And the kids knew that." He nodded to himself. "I wish I had his contacts. I figure maybe he was onto something and this time it caught up with him. Way we hear it this town's the delivery point for a lot of the stuff that gets burned, sniffed, and popped across the river."

"Would you know any of the kids who were particular friends of Ed's?"

"Not me. Not by name or face. Check your own juvenile records, Judge. Check Ed's. You might find some names from those. And if you do find something, then call me."

I shook my head. "Ed did a lot of his unofficial stuff in his head." But I thought I'd check. Maybe there was a record someplace.

He looked at me. "This isn't your line of work, Judge." He got out a cigar and carefully unwrapped it. He began to chew it without lighting. We stood close together, each thinking our individual dark thoughts.

"Ed never said any more than he had to say." He looked up at me. "You knew him better than anyone except maybe his half sister. He tell you anything?"

"No. I don't know anything about drug traffic or juvenile informers. I've had a lot of drug stuff in court, but it's been quiet for a while." I shook my head, remembering. "Sometimes we talked for hours when things were slow in court."

"Whoever killed Ed may believe that you're also a danger to them," he said softly.

"Ed had too many friends to count. I was just one of them."

"Nevertheless," he began . . .

"I really don't know a thing," I said.

"Well, if you hear anything or remember something which might be of help, I'd sure appreciate a call," he said stolidly. He looked at the women still crowding together around Mom's wheel chair. Then he looked at his watch. "Come on, wife."

"Me too."

"Did you hear about Chili Blackwell?" he asked.

I nodded.

"He'd be a damn fool to come around here." He shook his head. "Mean bastard. I got him one time. He strong-armed an old man who lived down along the river. Chili knew the old man had money hidden. He tied him to a chair and burned him all over with a cigarette butt. One of the neighbors heard something and called us. I made the run." He smiled gently, remembering. "He tried to resist arrest."

"That sounds like Chili all right."

He nodded. "All we could get him for it was a six months' trip. The old man ain't ever been the same. Prosecutor had to deal it because he couldn't or wouldn't testify—I forget which." He nodded again and said: "You did a good thing when you sent him off. Mean bastard."

"That's right."

"Watch out for him."

3

The City Over the River

Outside, pushing Mom, escorting Jen, I saw Randy Rumple. He's the only member of the party hierarchy who still speaks to me, probably because he's a lawyer and I see him day after day in court, possibly also because we've known each other a lifetime.

He greeted Mom and Jen effusively and then moved close to me.

"I need to talk to you sometime real soon."

"Sure. Why not now?" I asked.

"Not here. Too many people around. I'll call you and buy you a drink."

"All right."

We moved on past him to the car.

After we took Mom home, when she steadfastly refused to join us, Jen and I drove across the river to the city. The interstate arrowed through the smog of downtown. We found our exit and the restaurant we sought on south, fighting the almost unmanageable traffic.

Capio's Tavern is in an old and huge building with faded paint. Around the ramshackle, brick building the neighborhood has disintegrated so that, in the past few years, the owners have managed to buy sufficient parking area. We parked in the new lot. A uniformed black patrolman, moonlighting, recognized us vaguely as semi-regulars, probably because of Jen. He gave her a smile and a wave from his heated booth in the center of the lighted parking area. We waved back.

We went inside. Except for one, big, front room the old building was carved up inside like a Swiss cheese. There were at least two dozen small rooms off both sides of a central hall. Two floors like that. A waiter conducted us to one of the smaller rooms. There was just space for a table and a couple of chairs. The lights were low and the table was covered with a glistening cloth. Around the walls of the room there were frames containing old newspaper clippings, none newer than thirty years. Lindbergh flew the Atlantic, the bubble broke on Wall Street, Dewey beat Roosevelt.

The waiter brought us double martinis in huge tumblers and scurried away with our food orders.

"I heard that Ed didn't die where he was found," Jen said.

"Who told you that?" I asked curiously.

"A lady at the funeral home. I think she maybe works at the hospital. She was around when they were doing the autopsy."

"I heard the same thing from a policeman," I said, grinning. "It wasn't supposed to be for publication."

"Tiny Quinn," she said. "I saw you talking to him. I'd be careful of him. He and Amos used to be very close."

"Tiny seems okay."

"Maybe he is." She looked away and then back. "Ed isn't for us to worry about. The police will handle it."

"I know."

She leaned across the table, looked me in the eyes and then kissed me very lightly.

"Your mother is something else," she said.

I had a sudden intuition. "Was she on marriage tonight?"

She nodded. "She said I could move into the house and we could take over the second floor."

"In a lot of ways I'd like that."

"You can't just move out, Mickey."

"I know that. If I get re-elected I was thinking about perhaps building a cottage on the back of the lot." I looked at her. "I've tried to talk to her about that, but she doesn't hear me." I shook my head. "It just wouldn't be right to move you in with her. She runs things. She runs me."

"She needs you."

"I know. I don't want to declare independence from her. All I want is my own place. I want to build it and furnish it and decorate it—with you."

She nodded. "It might not be so bad on the second floor. And I'm getting along in years."

"All of twenty-seven," I said.

She ignored that. "When I worked for Amos he liked to

show me off like some sort of a prize cow. He'd never really say anything, but he'd bring his people out into my office and introduce them and then they'd go back into his office and I could hear them laughing in there. And I guess it's always been that way—even before Amos. Is it because I'm taller than most other girls?"

"Tall girls are very glamorous and mysterious," I said. "Particularly when they go out and in like you do on the way up and down."

She kicked me lightly and continued: "He paid me overtime for night work and I needed the money to live. I figured he was telling his associates that the relationship was more than a business one, but he was always a gentleman until that one night when he came back to the office sort of drunk. He made his move and I'd been waiting for it I guess. It didn't make any difference to him that he was married and far past fifty." She looked down at the tablecloth. "I kneed the son of a bitch good and quit. He called me and wanted me to come back. I guess I knew it would be more of the same. Then he tried to keep me from getting another job."

"My motives were pure of course," I said, grinning. "I hired you because of your shorthand. I only noticed the rest of you long thereafter."

She gave me a disbelieving smile.

She'd grown up in my town, six years after me. I'd never known her until she'd come defiantly into my office seeking work. That had been just at the time when old Miss Hattie had been insistent upon retirement. I'd hired Jen as an assistant without party approval when I couldn't get it. I'd moved her on up to court stenographer when Miss Hattie left to live with her widowed sister in Sarasota, Florida.

I knew Jen had been married once when she was very young, knew it because she'd told me. I knew she'd divorced him after two years and no children. I didn't know why. She'd never said and I had no desire to dig into it. I'd known her first husband very vaguely—like you know many people in a small town. I remembered him as a big time salesman for the local furniture factory who drank hard, lived hard, then moved on. Once she told me she'd not heard from him since the divorce. I'd not detected regret in her voice.

And I knew I wanted her on a permanent basis. But not just yet. Not without security, with maybe having to go back into the practice and fight it there, trying to keep Annie in school and Mom in therapists.

"Some of the people in the courthouse don't like you, Mickey. I hear it. They say you aren't a practical politician—that you should have given Amos bond and then this whole thing would have collapsed."

"I'm not very political. I'll admit not being that way. It's a disease I hope will get worse."

"Amos owns a lot of the newspaper stock." She nodded. "I've seen his dividend checks."

"I never read the local paper. The papers over here in the city do a better job covering our news. And besides, I like their comic pages."

"You're going to have to quit laughing at me," she said. "Lots of people in our town read the paper that's printed here. Amos's paper. Plus Amos runs the courthouse and controls the organization. He's mad at you mostly because

he got himself in trouble and because of me. Maybe if I
found another job it might work out. The jury will probably find him not guilty. There's only a circumstantial case
against him. Even the prosecutor admits that. Amos will
tell a plausible story and the jury will believe him. He can
be charming. No one knows how mean he is until they
cross him."

"Never," I said.

"You mean the jury finding Amos not guilty?"

"No. That might happen. Never count on a jury for
anything. I mean you quitting your job. You know he'd
chase you anyplace you went if you stayed in this area.
And I'm assuming that you would stay because I want
you here. And trying to placate him won't do any good.
When I denied his bond all of my chances went down the
drain right then."

"He might get over it," she said.

"No, again. The last thing he really got over was undoubtedly a childhood case of the whooping cough. Amos
is the kind of man who makes enemies and then, once he's
made them, keeps them forever. Besides, I feel more comfortable being his hate list. It makes me sure I'm on
the right road."

"He'll beat you, Mickey. One way or another he'll beat
you."

"Then I'll go back into practice."

"He can make it tough on you there, too," she said.
"He tells a lot of people what to do."

I smiled at her with a confidence I didn't feel.

"He doesn't tell us what to do," I said. I didn't add:
Mom does.

When I got home my eighteen-year-old sister, Anna, was still up. She had the door to her room open and her light was on. I walked on up there. She takes up most of the third floor. She was reading in bed when I stopped at her door. We live different schedules. I'm a day person and she's a night person.

"Hi, Annie."

"Your lipstick needs blotting," she said, looking me over critically. "If you keep going out with that big, gorgeous girl sooner or later she's going to entice you into the back seat and, bang, you'll get pregnant or something."

"How's school going?" I asked, pointedly ignoring her.

"Fine," she said. "I'm reading psychology. Right now I'm into odd birds and peculiar bees or something. Want to hear?"

I shook my head and examined her. She inherited the very best of Mom and Pop in looks. She is, at eighteen, startlingly beautiful, with huge, dark eyes and very black hair. So far the beauty hasn't bothered her a bit. I recalled that not too many years back she'd refused to give in to the already somewhat obvious fact that she was a girl. She'd dressed like a boy, played rough games with the boys in the neighborhood, and become pretty tough at those games. Then, about three years back, she'd blossomed and we'd endured an onslaught of lovesick ex-teammates and game opponents. Mom had fed them all and petted them impartially and Annie had now and then passed them a smile and a casual word. She still viewed the world around her in a detached way, closer to Mom and to me than she'd been to any outsider. She had yet to love.

She was bright and amiable and very self-able. She looked at the school world she lived in, with its large share of wild ones, with almost amusement. She could feel sorrow, want to help even, but nothing had hurt her yet. She'd been too young really to feel deeply the loss of Pop, and Mom was Mom, wheel chair or no.

I hoped that she was one of the charmed ones who sail through life with smiles all the way. No bad winds, no hurricanes, the sun perpetually out. Life is that way for a fortunate few.

"I'm sorry I didn't get to the funeral home," she said. "Did I tell you that Ed was over around the college a few days back?"

"Oh? What was he doing over around there?"

"I saw him in the coffee shop. It was during court hours so I thought maybe it was business of some kind. He was sitting with some guys. Just talking. He didn't see me. I've noticed him here and there on the campus before, so maybe it wasn't anything."

"Who were the boys?"

"Two guys with beards. I know that doesn't mean much because so many have beards. I don't know their names, but maybe I could find out. Is it important?"

"I don't know. If you can do it easily find out their names and let me know. And do it so that no one knows why you're asking."

She nodded. Her eyes sparkled like new wine. She loved intrigue.

"Again, don't indicate any real interest in them," I

warned. "Maybe just say you've seen them before and wondered who they were."

"But why?"

"Because the police seem to think Ed wasn't killed in a hit-run accident. Maybe he was killed investigating drugs, trying to get back to the main man. Someone might get edgy about you trying to dig around if they tied Ed to the boys you saw him with. I wouldn't want to chance that." I thought about it for a moment, worried about what she would do and the method she'd use doing it. "Maybe it would be best if we just forgot the whole thing."

"If I don't find out or can't find out, then what would you do?"

"I guess let the police in on it. That way Tiny Quinn would be asking the questions. I suppose that could be even worse."

She leaned toward me, dark eyes in shadow as they moved out of the direct light. She said: "You're not a bad older brother, Mickey, but you fool around in those old lawbooks so much that you're all small print—like them. You're an incurable stuff. You always want everything done in the proper manner like you do it in court and you're always worried about me." She nodded. "I'll get your names and no one will even remember I asked. Be better than some policeman going in there with me."

I smiled inwardly at her estimation of me. She was right. I was a lawyer and now a judge and my methods and reactions came predictably from that staid background. Sometimes the old Mickey Tostini peered through, the Tostini from Vietnam, from wild boyhood, but it was through a foot or so of dark glass. I sighed inaudibly. Too late to change. Born to Rotary, raised to small-town knighthood by the Chamber of Commerce.

She said: "Mom and I heard on the news that Chili Blackwell escaped from prison."

I nodded.

"Isn't he the mean one who used to parade up and down in front of the house before and during his trial?"

"Yes."

"He sounds like more to worry about than a couple of boys with beards."

"We know who Chili is. We don't know who's in back of the drugs—who the main man is." I looked at her. "Do you remember last year when I tried so many drug cases?"

She nodded.

"We had fourteen convictions. All jury trials. All defended by first-class lawyers. In every case we offered the defendant the chance to draw a suspended sentence if he could help us back to the source of the drugs." I shook my head. "We never got anyplace."

"Maybe they just didn't know."

"Some of them had to know. But no one told us a thing. They were more afraid of what could happen to them if they talked to us than they were of prison. We've had three more cases this year. Same way."

She thought for a minute. "Did you lock the house up?" she asked.

"Yes. I locked up." I looked at her and I could see she was worried a little. "No one will bother us," I said. "If they tried to get at me there would be a lot of heat and

that would be very bad for business. So don't worry. I'm
not expecting any personal problems."

"All right," she said, but her voice was funny.

I tilted her chin up and gave her a quick kiss on the
nose and, after a moment, she laughed and was all right
so I headed back down for my own room.

Inside that room, Mom, in her periodic forays into the
hinterlands above the first floor, had kept all as once it
had been. The room was still a place of fraternity pad-
dles, scout certificates, pictures of a boy football player
who somewhat resembled me. There was also one picture
of me in uniform, poised ferociously, semi-automatic
weapon at ready, silver bar gleaming on shoulder, under a
hot, tropic sun.

At least she'd put away the Teddy bear. But the things
of my adulthood weren't kept here. They were in my
office at the courthouse or in other rooms, downstairs. Not
here.

I had a sudden realization that if I married Jen and
brought her here that Mom would still insist on keeping
this room as it had been for a very long time. She'd do it
by force of will, by arguing longer than you cared to
debate, by stubbornly replacing that which you hid away.
I nodded to myself. Mom had a lot of good points. It was
just that she wished to freeze us all into the mold she'd
built for herself, the mold that said that one day she'd rise
from her wheel chair and Pop would come back through
the front door. If she could keep it all as it had been before that fatal day, then there was a chance. It was a fantasy, a dream, but it was her dream. She could be practi-

cal and still have that dream. Practicality and the dream were separate worlds.

I hung my good suit carefully on its hanger, undid the prosthetic hand and shrugged it off, and gave it up for the night.

But on this night sleep was not easily come by. I kept tossing and turning and remembering my last words with Ed Long.

He'd been my father's friend and then he'd been my friend. He'd helped clear my political way. I'd had my first appointment as zoning board attorney because of him. And later, when I took the bench, I'd asked him out of his bored, semi-retirement to be my combination bailiff, probation officer. He'd come willingly. That was the first time I got crosswise with Amos Walker, but I'd made the appointment anyway. And Ed had been good at the job—as I'd known he'd be.

I got to the last time I'd seen him, three days back now. It had been after a long day of jury examination by prosecution and defense.

Ed had stood in front of the bench and smiled his gentle smile, a smile without cynicism, a smile untouched by the dirty years as sheriff.

"You ought to know you're getting cut up badly downstairs," he said. The courtroom had emptied and we were alone.

"That figures. What I really don't understand is *why?* If Amos didn't want me to be the judge in his case, he could have removed me with a very simple motion for a change of venue. He didn't. And now all I've got to do is make sure he gets as fair a trial as he can be given."

"That ain't the way of it, Mickey. Amos, and probably Amos's lawyer, thought the prosecutor was being stupid when he left you on the bench. Here you are, top of the ticket, up for election to a job he let you get appointed into. That makes you *his*, Mickey. Then you wind up not admitting him to bail, not finding some technical reason in all the motions he filed to throw the whole thing out. Amos don't want a fair trial. He wants what he considers his dues from you. I've talked to him—if you could call it a talk. Him cussin' and me listening."

"There's a clear case against him, Ed. Sure it's circumstantial, but I'm not supposed to determine his guilt or innocence in a bond hearing. And I'm not supposed to give bond where the evidence was like it was in the hearing—it's as simple as that. You sat through most of it. What did you think?"

"I think he killed his little bitch wife, but so what? If I wanted to commit political suicide, I'd have done as you did. Of course I'm already politically dead anyway, so my opinion only comes from experience. Amos is a very direct man. Ask me as the expert who's rubbed him wrong. He helped you get where you are—or at least he didn't stand in your way. To him that's the alpha and the omega."

"Tough. It shouldn't be. He helped me get here to do a job and I'm doing that job. He helped me because the others on the governor's list looked worse to him. He helped me because he's party chairman, county and district, and getting people appointed is part of the job."

He shook his head, grinning. "Ain't that way to him, Mickey. To him you're a bug. He's the boss and you're his hireling. And now he's got the word out and he's got his people filing in and out of that jail talking to him every night. They're switching to the honorable Perry L. Bobbin. Perry didn't have much of a chance when he filed before the bond hearing, but now he'll beat you blue in a couple of weeks even if the town out there knows he's a loud-mouthed clodhopper who sits around counting the rhinestones in his old college fraternity pin." He nodded seriously. "Now me, I'll help you when and where I can. But that's strictly on one condition."

"What's the condition?"

"That I get bond," he said and brayed laughter. It took him a while to stop laughing, but when he did he continued: "I know some unlikely places where I can dig up support—places where I've got more on them than Amos has."

"How about Gosport?"

"He'll stay out. He won't hurt you, but he won't help you. I asked already."

"Thanks, Ed."

4

Final Rites

In the morning all was foggy through the first two cups of black coffee. Mom was solicitous with me.

"You aren't sleeping good, Mickey. I heard you call out during the night. Maybe I should ask Doc Luby to give you some mild sleeping pills."

"I'm okay, Mom." I thought about Chili Blackwell being loose. "No pills."

She wheeled her chair back and forth, watching me out of the corner of her eye, not satisfied.

"Your sister will make sure I get to the funeral on time. You have to be there early as one of the pallbearers. There'll be a lot of people there. Why don't you wear your hook?"

"Not today, Mom."

"That's a very striking girl you've got," she said, changing her angle of attack.

"Thank you. She thinks you're a doll also. A mutual admiration society."

"You should bring her around here more often so as to get used to it," she said, dimpling with pleasure.

"That's a nice idea," I said, not liking it. I gulped down what was left of the coffee and fled to the door. She rolled after me for one final inspection.

"Your top shirt button is unfastened," she said. "Lean down here."

I did and she buttoned it. It was too tight and that was why I hadn't buttoned it before. Using the stub or my false hand I've become pretty adept at buttoning and can mostly do it without help.

A few blocks down the street I pulled to the side and undid the button and loosened my taut tie a little. I sighed with relief and drove on. I turned on the radio and heard another ad for my opponent, then a sad country western song wherein the singer sought forgiveness from his lady friend. I didn't hear it out to see if she gave him what he was seeking. She might forgive him, but I could not and turned him off.

"Half-a-man" waited for me near my parking spot in back of the courthouse. He sat in the cool, sunless morning in his cart, his one good hand covered with a thick, dirty glove, the rest of him shiny clean.

He likes people to believe he's a war victim, but he isn't. That deceit is one of his few vanities. He was born shy one leg and one arm. His remaining arm is all right, but the leg is stunted, yet strong.

He owns a Byronic head covered with soft-appearing ringlet curls, blue-black in color. He has a strong, beaked nose and carved, quite prominent lips. It's a face at the near edge of beauty. Because the face is surrounded by its edifice of ruined body few notice it.

His real name is George Jones. He has no middle name, not even a middle initial. Perhaps his father and mother, seeing his complications at birth, decided against any complicated name. No one calls him by his real name now and I suspect he'd probably not know to answer if someone did use that name. He is now "Half-a-man," or just "Half." And because he's rational he's adopted that name for himself and takes no offense to it.

He's also adopted me. Perhaps the original adoption took place because of my missing hand. Perhaps it was aided because I've found him out—know that despite the fact that he drinks that he also reads and thinks. His tastes are very catholic. He can quote whole passages from Shakespeare and he's a completist on Harlan Ellison. He likes Steinbeck, but prefers Dick Francis and/or John D. MacDonald. All this is something he hides carefully from the courthouse-wall world around him.

Each morning he hovers in wait for me and bums me for a dollar. It's my admission fee to the courthouse. Five dollars a week. He disdains working on Saturdays. Fifty-two weeks a year, assuming I take no vacation. Two hundred sixty dollars.

For payment he tells me things. Those things he tells me are not normally what I care about knowing, but I always listen gravely. I know, for example, that Samdog Cabel, a noted psycho-drunk and Half's good friend, once was a promising concert violinist. I know that Annie Bay, a redheaded high roller who sets up unsuspecting itinerants with bank rolls in bust-out card games, passes on a percentage of her earnings to her mother, which would be more laudable if the older Bay lady wasn't mostly in the same business as Annie. I know that Sharper Jackman hasn't worked a day since Pearl Harbor and that his wife, Kateet, gives him fifty dollars a week just to stay away from home. She suffers, according to Half, from religious scruples which won't allow her to seek a divorce, but do allow her to take just about anyone to bed with her she can talk into it.

"Mornin', Half," I said.

He condescended enough to give me a cool nod. He's been a little aloof since my political fortunes worsened. Perhaps he can foresee a future time when he'll need to break in a new donor.

"You're losing ground," he advised. He accepted his daily dollar with dignity and pocketed it. "It could be all over."

"How's that?"

"I hear it from everyone," he said. "The gents out there on the courthouse wall say you're probably going to get your butt beat. And you know that Samdog Cabel ain't been wrong about an election in thirty years."

Samdog had also never failed to get his five dollars and a pint in exchange for his vote, I remembered, but I said nothing. And most people who are "always right" about elections are right in retrospect. It's easy to pick winners after the fact.

"You think that it would just be best if I withdrew?" I asked.

He gave me a look full of worry. I was vocalizing his deepest fear.

I continued mercilessly: "I mean if everyone has me beat already?"

He rolled a little away, the better to see me. He's never developed much of a sense of humor and he can't be sure when I'm joking.

"You still got a good chance," he said. "Me'n Samdog are working for you—hard."

"Thanks a lot, Half."

We nodded at each other, good friends again. I moved on. At the double doors of the courthouse Samdog Cabel watched with hooded eyes. He's insane, but not committably so. He believes the world around him is in constant plot against him and so he drinks. I suppose I'm part of the plot. Only Half completely escapes it. He loves Half in his alcohol-damaged way. On some of his really foggy days I've heard other of the wall sitters say he even doubts Half, but not much, not enough.

He said deferentially to me as I passed: "The world's a dirty prostitute, Your Honor." His voice was very good, deep and rich. When you heard it you could believe there had once been music in the man.

I nodded. An answer would only bring the same statement forth again. It was his greeting to all.

———◆———

Upstairs, when things got underway, we picked away at one more juror who seemed fairly secure in that his answers were reasoned. I thought we might make it soon.

I'd presided at three first degree murder trials during

my time as judge. Except for excessive newspaper coverage those trials had seemed little different from the twenty plus other jury trials I'd had—mostly drug cases. Perhaps, in the murder trials, the lawyers were a little more in earnest, a fraction better prepared.

I noticed that Amos kept glaring up toward me on the bench and whispering things to his lawyer. I decided that last night's events at the funeral home had undoubtedly been relayed to Amos, perhaps with some embellishment.

When the juror the lawyers were examining had survived the worst of the questioning I halted things. I warned the jury panelists about what they should and should not do as probable jurors and turned them loose for the weekend. They went out happily.

Higer followed close behind me to my chambers.

"My client claims you've been discussing his case and your attitude about it in public," he said belligerently, with a rehearsed frown that made the eyebrows even more apparent.

"No, I have not."

"He says he can show you have been."

"Then if your client can convince some appellate tribunal up the line that I've committed some kind of error he might be able to get the case reversed." I smiled. We both knew that what he was complaining about wasn't appealable. If I was prejudiced that was my right—as long as I wasn't prejudiced in court.

"He'd like his relief now," Higer said. "He wants you off the bench—another judge."

"The time for filing such a motion has long since passed, Mr. Higer. Surely you're aware of that?"

"Nevertheless . . ."

". . . No nevertheless, Mr. Higer. Your client will get his fair trial here. But that's all he's going to get."

As I was making my last statement Prosecuting Attorney Allen Dunwich entered the door. He looked from Higer to me, then back, not comprehending.

Higer sniffed contemptuously at both of us, pushed roughly past Dunwich and exited my chambers.

"Now that's what I call a high dudgeon," Dunwich said.

I nodded. "Gloves are off, Al. I think it's finally sifted all the way through that I'm not and never will be one of the good old boys and that I won't trade favors to be elected judge."

Al grinned. "Never fear. Someplace on high the moving finger is writing that you aren't buyable."

"I just haven't heard the right offer yet."

"Sure," he said. "Tell me the one about the tooth fairy, too." He leaned a little toward me. "I want you to think about something. Perry L. Bobbin filed against you before you ruled on bond in this case. He's running a well-funded campaign. You can't listen to the radio without hearing a dozen of his jingles, you can't pick up the paper without seeing his smiling picture. So someone was trying to get you out before your problems with Amos Walker." He nodded. "And who have we been roughest on?"

I didn't say anything, but I knew he was thinking back to the drug cases we'd had.

"You get elected again and maybe some one of those guys who are doing five hard years up at state prison may change his mind about giving us some information," Al said.

"What's my election got to do with it?"

"You convicted them. What if your successor in office decided to let the most of them out on shock probation?"

"You're too devious in the head, Al. The sellers we sent up didn't talk because they were more scared of what could happen to them if they did talk than having to go to prison."

"Maybe. But Perry's a clown. Cheap to elect, cheap to keep thereafter. And I hear things in my office. I know he's getting some money from the drug people. Oh sure, they clean it up before it gets to him, but that's the source."

"If you hear things like that maybe you also hear who the main local man is?"

"I hear too many names. I hear Amos. I hear Judge File. I hear Sheriff Zisk." He nodded. "My bet's Zisk. One reason those people might be so afraid is knowing that they might be in his jail."

————◆————

After the funeral Jen and I went, in company with others, to the Elks Club. There, with Allen Dunwich and a few other assorted pallbearers, we conducted our own private wake. A consensus was quickly reached that Ed had been "a good man." Not much to leave, but better than some. We sat at a big round table and drank and told "Ed" stories.

The Elks bar is usually referred to as the "horse barn." Some early member, enchanted by Twenty Grand, War

Admiral, and Kentucky Bourbon, bought dozens of pictures of horses bedecked with roses and strung the pictures at strategic intervals around the club walls. In looking the place over, the curious viewer has the immediate urge to drink deeply and so avoid the ghostly thunder of concentrated hoofs.

The crowd soon dwindled down to Jen and me, plus Allen and wife, whom he'd dutifully called. She'd not attended the funeral.

"To Ed," Al said for the half-dozenth time. He raised a wavering glass. "Why in hell he'd go out of his way to try to feed information to that two-faced sheriff is beyond me."

"Guess about it, Al?"

He concentrated. "Bad as he disliked and distrusted Zisk he hated sale druggies worse." He leaned forward. "He really did despise the professionals. Not the kids who wind up caught like flies in molasses, but the hard ones we've made a try at clearing out, the ones who make a living at the trade."

Jen said conversationally: "There's got to be a lot of money in it."

Al nodded at her. "Yep. And someone up high is taking a king's share of it." He shook his head wryly. "When I get all done with this damned job in a couple of years, when some incompetent retires me, I'll bet I really haven't scratched the surface or left even a ripple behind."

"There are a lot of people you've convicted and I've sentenced," I said.

"Means nothing, Judge. Plenty of those around." He looked moodily into his glass. "And to change the subject,

I'll bet that when I get done picking that jury there are going to be at least three people on it who, unknown to me, owe Amos Walker one arm and one leg." He lowered the glass and sipped from it.

Ellie, his wife, finished her drink. She sat it down and leaned closer to Jen and, together, they ignored us and engaged in low-voiced girl talk.

"You watch Amos, Judge," Al said, as low-voiced as the girls were. "He's the kind who'll eventually use muscle to get what he wants."

"Not this time, Al. He comes after me that way and it gets to be public knowledge and then maybe it hurts his candidate for judge."

"That wouldn't be something he'd even bother to think about," Al said. "He's on trial for first degree murder. Granted, we're not asking for the death penalty, but we seldom do or can these days. He'll pull every stop. Any conviction is too much for him. When you didn't set him a bond and let him get out to manipulate and maneuver, you hurt him badly. That's going to prey on him worse and worse as time goes on and as the trial proceeds." He nodded, thinking. "I've got a few policemen I can trust. I'm going to have them keep an eye on you and yours until this thing is completed. Besides, Chili Blackwell is out someplace. I heard a report he'd been spotted in the north part of the county. We found nothing."

"As far as Chili's concerned there's no need to guard me unless you guard all his jurors," I said.

He smiled and nodded. "He hates you worse, Judge. And you should never turn down aid. If you refused it and I let you, then both of us might regret it—me for the rest of my life."

With that chilling statement he stopped my argument. Before I could think of another objection, he had hailed the waitress for reinforcements and the dinner menu.

———————◆◆———————

In the morning, after a sodden, dreamless night, I took a lengthy shower, hot, then cold, then hot again. I drank a full can of V-8 juice and three cups of black coffee while Mom watched me silently. I knew what she was thinking. I drank too much on Fridays. The rest of the week was under control, but Friday was release day—end of the week and its crisis areas.

I drove to the courthouse and darted through a pile of backed-up paper work, inheritance tax orders, final reports in estates, judgments, mail which had stacked up. I did what I could and put aside that which would have to wait until the trial was done.

It was Saturday and the courthouse was dark and empty around me. Outside the weather had warmed some. Tornado season. Three years back a huge band of tornados, after years of false alarms, had flown up the river and attacked the city across the river and my town ravenously, chewing up neighborhoods, destroying all that lay in the way. Contempt was dead. The area was now tornado aware. From my dirty window I could see the farmers set up around the square for their Saturday market watch the sky carefully. I'd heard their talk when I entered the courthouse. Last year had been too dry for them, this year had been too wet.

My area had all things. Tonight, if I wanted, I could

cross the river, eat a gourmet dinner, then attend live opera. Or I could drive ten miles north, park my car, and move away from the road. A hundred yards from that road the land was pretty much as it had been when the first settlers came into the country. The land would always be there, but with the continuing errors of men, the city might not be.

I carried the accumulation of signed papers out and put them on the tiny elevator to the clerk's office. I went back and sat again in my chair and watched the farmers below.

The phone rang. I let it ring for a while, debating about whether or not to answer it. It persisted and so finally I picked it up.

"Hello," I said.

Nothing.

"Judge's office," I said.

Still nothing.

"Who's there?" I asked.

No answer, but I could detect sound. Breathing?

I hung the phone up. I've had calls of a similar nature before. It's a thing I've learned to live with. Cranks—nuts. Getting even for something you've done or they think you've done.

In a few minutes the phone rang again.

"Hello," I said.

Nothing again. Breathing maybe.

I opened up a side desk drawer and dropped the telephone receiver in it and sat there for a moment trying to count up the crank calls I'd had. They were almost beyond number. Most had talked, some few had threatened.

A psychiatrist once told me that such callers were usually harmless, persons afraid to face you directly.

Usually.

I went on back to what had been Ed Long's office. Since the trial had begun, the two special bailiffs I'd employed had been using it for break periods, but it was still Ed's office. At least to me.

He had a big, metal roll file by his desk and I thumbed through the Manila folders in it. Much of what was in the files was new territory to me, things I'd never seen, situations Ed had handled without me. That was as it should be. A good probation officer uses his judge as little as possible.

Many of the names on the files were names I didn't recognize. Some I did know as probationers. Kids in trouble.

I remembered that Ed had once said to me: "In these times, Judge, show me a kid who hasn't been into some kind of problem and I'll show you a kid who was either born lucky, has a quick bicycle, or who's maybe mentally deficient."

I didn't believe it was quite that way, but we live close up on each other in these restless years. The chance to be caught is greater, the temptations are more apparent.

I spent an hour going through the files, but there was nothing that reached right out and grabbed at me. I paid particular attention to drug cases. There were lots of them, but then there are most places these days. Teen-aged addicts, teen-aged pushers. A whole new industry to take the place of the jobs that have vanished with the automation winds.

But nothing in the files seemed to be a clue to Ed's death.

When I was done with the files I went through his desk drawers. Inside there was a collection of items from Ed's long life—an album of old photos, a half-finished packet of stomach mints, circulars from homes for delinquent boys and girls, letters he'd deemed important enough to save, but not to file.

His appointment book seemed to have vanished. I couldn't find it. I was almost sure he kept one, or at least had kept one in the past.

I thumbed through the photo album. It was very old, from back before the time when I knew Ed or knew of him. Some of the faces in the pictures seemed vaguely familiar, as if I'd seen faces like them, but long afterward. Or perhaps the children of those faces. The people in the photos were dressed in clothes that were from a time I also couldn't exactly place—maybe forty years back. The only person I could for sure recognize was Ed. In one picture he was standing by another young man who seemed very familiar. I was pretty sure the companion was Amos Walker, or Amos's brother or father? I went back to my own office and looked. Amos was sixty-one years old and Ed had been sixty-two. So, if the picture was of Amos, then the age would be right for it to be him and not his father or brother.

So what?

I shrugged and decided to take the album along. I carried it with me, walked back to my office and rehung the phone, and went to the elevator. Behind me, as I went

down the dark hall, the phone began to ring again. *This
one had patience.*

I drove home.

I put the album in the front closet atop a shelf there.
Upstairs I could hear Anna singing a pop tune in her very
good soprano voice.

I went on out to the sunroom and found Mom. She had
her nose in a book. On its garish, paper cover a beautiful
girl, clad all in white (what little there was of it), fled
into a dark cemetery. Behind the frightened girl one lone
light shone from the upper window of a huge, forbidding
house. Mom loved Gothic novels.

The house on the paperback cover reminded me of our
house.

I stood patiently in front of her wheel chair until she
decided to notice me.

I said: "I talked to Annie a little last night, but I want
both of you to be extra careful over the next few days.
Open the door to no one you don't know. And you might
say something to Annie about being very careful of people she doesn't know for a while." I shook my head.
"When I say something to her she thinks I'm just a
stuffed shirt and overcautious."

"What's happened now?" Mom questioned.

"Nothing, nothing," I said, not meeting her eyes. "It's
just a warm trial. And it will get warmer. I wouldn't want
anyone to get the idea of pressuring me through you—
either of you. It's been tried before and these are peculiar times. Best way for things to go right is for you and
Annie to be on your guard." I thought for a moment.
"Then there's a man who has cause to hate me—us—who
escaped prison a couple of days ago."

"Chili Blackwell?" she asked.

"Would you recognize him?"

"Of course. He walked up and down in front of the house often enough. And your father knew him."

Pop knew everyone. I waited.

She finally nodded. "All right then. But I want to show you something." She rolled away.

I followed dutifully.

She separated a curtain a fraction away from a living room window. I followed her glance. A nondescript, late-model car was parked on the far side of the street. I'd not noticed it when I drove up. A man was hunched low in the front seat. I recognized him. City police.

"He's all right," I said.

"There was another one there earlier," she said. "And when I got up this morning I thought I saw that deputy sheriff go past outside real slow."

"Joe Pierceton?"

She nodded. "Why are all of them watching the house?"

"Because I've got this murder trial going. Because Chili's out," I said with some irritation.

"And Amos is in," she mused, not offended.

"Yes."

She shrugged. "Well, your father always said Amos was the nastiest of men. I'll warn Anna and we'll try to be more careful." She looked up at me. "And you be careful too, son. If someone wants to hurt one of us, they'd most probably prefer you."

I nodded.

She watched me and then dismissed it. There was nothing she could do and so she would ignore it.

"I've got some ham salad I made for lunch," she said, going on to more important things. "Will you be at home this afternoon?"

"For a while. I've got a Legion meeting. And remember that Jen's invited for dinner tonight. You invited her. We can eat in or out. Annie's invited out also if she wants to go along."

"We'll eat here of course," she pronounced firmly. "And Anna will eat with us. She said she was staying in tonight and studying." She shook her head. "That girl. Boys call for dates by the dozens and she stays in on a Saturday night." She stopped. "Is there enough to drink in the house?"

"I'll pick up some wine and a bottle of Early Times at the liquor store on my way home from the Legion meeting," I said.

She leaned a little toward me, working the right wheel of her chair with strong, impatient fingers. "Wear your ribbon lapel button, son."

I put it on for her to see, but then I removed it when I left the house. An old war I wanted to forget. Too many good men I'd known were dead so that memories of those years were inhabited by ghosts, by familiar faces not to be seen again, by bad dreams.

Sometimes I wished my whole generation had made its way to Canada and Sweden and other ports of refuge.

Maybe the day will come when I hang about other old soldiers at parties and around bars and tell war stories, but I suspect that alcohol will have severely damaged my brain by then.

5

Legion

In front of the Legion home there is an artillery piece anchored in cement. On fine summer days kids play games upon it and around it, aping their idiot elders with young wars.

Inside, those elders play more advanced games with unknown rules. The Legion bar has become locally famous because so many marriages can trace the beginnings of their breakup to there. The management keeps it dark and cozy in the barroom. Men bring their wives. "Auxiliary cards" are provided. The men play cards in the stag rooms and drink too much. Some prowlers drink very little and move about carefully among the women. And things happen.

In addition to the famous bar, which is huge, the rest of the old, enormous once-residence has been divided into stag rooms, offices, meeting rooms.

I parked in the lot reserved for members. There were already quite a number of other cars parked there. Most of them probably hadn't been parked there for their owners to attend the meeting, but for the bar and the cardrooms. I walked past them in the wet gravel and entered the building by inserting my key card in the lock and buzzing it open.

I found my way through the darkness of the barroom and ordered a healing drink. The bar was crowded with both male and female patrons. A jukebox played kinky music and the laughter and conversation sounds mostly overwhelmed it. I nodded and smiled, remembering Gosport's advice. Some failed to return the courtesies. The Legion post is inhabited by many who are politically aware.

At two o'clock I went upstairs for the meeting. There seemed to be a larger crowd than was usual and, looking around, I found the reason.

My primary opponent ten days' hence was there. He was wearing his Legion button. A man I knew as one of Amos's sublieutenants had him in tow.

Perry L. Bobbin was dapperly dressed. He had on a bright tie which went well with his expensive jacket. His pants were knife-creased, impeccable. His shoes reflected the ceiling lights. Although he enjoys a reputation as a very sharp dresser among the members of the bar he is conceded to be its weakest member. I've heard him brag that he hasn't read a case since his graduation from law school twenty plus years back.

"Hi, Perry," I said cheerily, when he got close to me.

We shook hands gingerly.

"Hard on the campaign trail, I see," he said, eying me with ill-concealed distaste. We've never liked each other. I heard he was upset when I was appointed.

"Of course," I said. "And this is the first time I've seen you here for a meeting. Can I assume you plan to become active?"

"Could be," he said. He regarded me coolly for another moment until his guide hustled him on. Perry followed on around the room, shaking hands vigorously, smiling his hundred-watt smile.

I thought perhaps I ought to emulate him and go around the room shaking hands and smiling, but a sudden, unexpected attack of common sense stopped me. I couldn't out-politick anyone and for me to attempt it would be silly. All the people in this room already knew me. Hopefully I'd get most of their votes.

I stayed where I was and, soon, the meeting began.

That night, after I'd taken Jen home and said a lingering good night, I went carefully around our big house. The telephone calls of that morning were still on my mind. Chili Blackwell was on my mind. So was Amos Walker. I buttoned the old house up as tight as such could be done. I checked all windows to see that they were locked. I inspected back door and front door, side doors, and the cellar double door.

Outside, when I went to a window, the police watcher had either ended it for the time or had secreted himself. But, as I looked, I saw a sheriff's car drive slowly past, lights off. It stopped for a moment and the inner dome light went on. A smiling Joe Pierceton nodded at me and I waved at him. He blacked the car out and moved it on slowly.

Dinner had been a qualified success. Mom and Jen worked hard during it trying to indicate how much they appreciated each other. Annie winked and kicked me painfully a couple of times under the table while that performance was going on. Everyone but me fought over who was to do the dishes and Mom, as usual, won. Later we watched commercials about miracle detergents and pimple removers which civilization could not survive without. They were interspersed with short segments of a movie about a girl who'd done wrong, but who'd repented. It was a full four-handkerchief success with the ladies. I napped a little.

When I was done checking the house I went to bed, but it was difficult to find sleep. The old house creaked in the spring winds.

Then, finally, sleep came.

And I dreamed.

I dreamed I was back in the deep green jungle again, back in that desperate time when all of wanting was the desire to stay alive.

I dreamed of the dirty little men in black. Once again the grenade came into our midst and I screamed and scrambled for it and threw it, too late for me, but not too late for others.

I came awake. I remembered what the hospital corpsman had said—that the grenade had been defective or I wouldn't have lived—that other men lost hands without problems—that I should look on the good side.

I clenched my right hand. It was inordinately strong, so that I had to be careful sometimes in using it. Outside I could now hear rain. I was soaked with sweat. My vanished lower left hand and arm below the stub hurt again as they had hurt long ago. I had night problems with an old difficulty—thinking, or trying to think, of myself as a whole man. I'd been damaged. That time had passed. Hadn't it? The psychological problems had been worse for me than the loss of flesh and bone. For a very long time I'd pushed at myself to stay in the twilight, catch no more grenades, do nothing more that could cause harm and/or damage. The grenade had taught me that I was vulnerable, the loss had shown me that I must some day die. It had made me rabbit wary, unwilling to get into the main part of the fight. Sometimes, at times like this, on awakening, I could even admit to myself that such was what had made my law practice unsuccessful and that being judge had pushed me back into the fight and so been therapeutic.

I came all the way up from sleep. Around me there was something wrong, a subtle thing, but wrong. I tested it against normal. A sound? A feel? A smell?

I got up and shrugged on my robe and padded carefully out of my bedroom to check things again. The feeling was strong enough that I went to a downstairs closet and took out Pop's double-barreled 12 gauge. I checked it to see if it was loaded. It was and I moved on, holding it in my right hand, stub held ready to lay it over.

The windows seemed all right and so did the first floor doors. I went down to the basement after flicking on the light at the top of the stairs. It was a dim light and it created mostly shadows. Every corner was an alien land. I was sweating again.

There were traces of water underneath the double doors that led into the yard. The wet spots continued on into the basement. The thing which had set me off upstairs was stronger down here. It was a thing of smell.

Each pillar that rose to hold up the house, each dark wall, seemed to be a likely place where an invader could hide. The shotgun was a warm and comforting friend.

Nothing. *Come and gone.*

The telltale water drops led me to the furthest corner of the basement. Hidden in shadows there was an ancient gas stove, many years old. Once it had been used to heat water for washing in a less comfortable, but safer time. If there was a pilot light it had been sealed long ago.

One burner was turned on. I twisted the metal knob back to "off" position and the faint hissing stopped. There didn't seem to be enough of an accumulation yet to do real harm, but I opened the two closest basement windows and let the breeze further clear it away. When the smell was gone I closed the windows again. I stuffed an old broom handle through the under metal brackets of the suspect double doors. It could be dislodged, but I thought the dislodging would cause much noise.

I checked the rest of the basement, but there was nothing else. I relocked the windows.

As I reached the first floor the phone began to ring.

I remembered the tiny Santas I'd seen in store windows at Christmas past. They tapped windows with pointers and turned pages for shoppers to read. *See me. See me.*

I picked up the phone.

"Hello," I said.

Nothing. But someone was there.

After a time I hung the phone back up. It didn't ring again for the rest of the night, although I waited.

Some of the instincts I'd acquired by war remained within me. I could remember too well the jungle days, watching, moving slowly. The careless died. So sometimes did the non-careless. Some of those dead were better people than I'd ever be, but I was still alive.

Someone out there had given me warning. The gas jet on and the break-in had been meant to warn me, frighten me. Thinking about Mom and Annie it did frighten me.

I took the shotgun up and put it carefully in my closet. A good, close-up weapon. I'd had one in the jungle, despite regulations. Far better and more effective than the .45 caliber issue automatics.

———◄◆►———

In the morning I loaded Mom and Annie into the car and we went to Mass. Sometimes, these days, I wondered what I was doing there other than doing something the community desired, plus remaining with old habits. It wasn't that all belief was gone. There was enough old country peasant blood in me that such would never be. But sometimes I wondered about all churches as continuing institutions, about the 90 per cent that hung below the surface, the church clubs, the bingos, the frantic push for money.

This being an election year I did my wondering privately and silently.

Outside, when we made it back out into the pleasant

spring sun, Gosport McFay waited. He raised his hat to
the ladies. One side of his jaw was suspiciously large. I
wondered if he'd chewed in church. There are those who
swear Gosport's learned how to chew tobacco now without ever having to rid himself of the end product.

"How do, Mrs. Tostini and Miss Ann," he said, completely deadpan. "I wonder if I could borrow the judge
from you for a couple of minutes?"

"You certainly can, Gosport," Mom said severely. "We
can get by very well without him. He was sleeping in
church—and with the primary election only a little over a
week away."

Annie gave Gosport a look. She's not partial to him,
maybe because of the chewing tobacco. She took Mom's
wheel chair from me and rolled it on toward the car without a backward look. Gosport drew me confidentially
aside.

"You know what they're saying about you now, don't
you?" he asked.

I shook my head, preparing to be both frustrated and
appalled. Pre-election stories are uniformly vicious, as if
told by lovers who've fallen out.

"They're saying around that Ed was deep into the drug
scene and you with him. That's why you gave him his job
and why he wound up getting killed."

I shook my head. "That one's so tall the truth will catch
up with them on it, Gosport."

He shook his head. "All they got to do is confuse some
extra people with it between now and a week from Tuesday."

"What can I do?" I asked, frustration setting in hard.

Gosport shrugged. "Maybe ask the prosecutor for a grand jury to determine the source of the story. If they's one thing you've done it's get on the druggies." He watched me out of wise, old eyes. "You think maybe you could get Prosecutor Dunwich to call you a grand jury?"

"Maybe, but it would take too long. By the time the jurors were drawn by the jury commissioners, notified by the clerk, and it all got underway the primary would be over. And besides I wouldn't want to ask Dunwich to call a grand jury on something like that."

Gosport shook his head in agreement. The grand jury had been pie in the sky and both of us knew it. Swift retaliation. "Makes you damned mad though, don't it, boy?" he asked.

I nodded.

"They got enough going without making Ed look bad," he said softly. He looked up at me. "I told you I knew where they buried the bodies. I'm going to unearth you a few. And I'm going to come out for you." He shook his head at my look. "Don't count on it doing much. Just because I've walked on the water and beat old Amos a time or two don't mean I can carry someone on my back. We might both drown."

"I realize that," I said gratefully. "But I really appreciate you helping me. I'd about given it up."

"You got you a chance," he said. "There's just a whole lot of people ain't saying nothing. Trouble is you need them all." He cackled a little to himself and looked slyly up at me. "I heard you had some company at your Legion meeting yesterday."

"That's right."

"That Perry Bobbin. He's enough to gag a horse." He gave me another upward look, this one full of mischief. "How'd you like to go somewhere with me and hurt him a lot worse than he hurt you?"

"I'd like it."

"The last big meeting is tomorrow night at headquarters. I'll come on by your house and pick you up and we'll go there together."

"If you get that open about helping me it could hurt you in the future," I said doubtfully.

He shrugged. "I don't give a damn. I'll be past and pick you up tomorrow night. Seven o'clock. You be ready and waiting."

"All right," I said. I put out my hand and touched his shoulder. "Thanks, Gosport."

He was embarrassed for both of us.

"You heard any more about Ed?" I asked, at least partly to change the subject.

He said: "It's curious. There just ain't much going on it now. The police are going through the motions, but they's really only one man on it and they keep him busier than a one-armed paper hanger." He glanced at my false hand, colored, and said: "Excuse me."

I smiled at him. Once it would have been impossible to do so.

"Tiny Quinn?" I asked.

"He's the one, Mickey. I hear he's probably a half honest one, but I also hear he's so busy he ain't very swift at getting things done. And I hear it won't get better. Lots of things happen in this town. Them police assign him everything they can't figure out easy, and maybe that's only like 90 per cent of it. But he's got an assistant who helps. I know that one too. Amos got him on the police force. He couldn't catch cold." He shook his head ruefully, perpetually amazed at the perfidy and dry rot that surrounded him. "But I guess they have figured out that Ed wasn't killed where they found his body."

I nodded.

He'd saved something back. "Have you heard where they're saying Ed *was* killed?"

"No." Like most persons holding political office I either got information very quickly or very late—mostly the latter.

"I thought maybe you had. It's all over. Ed's supposed to have gotten it in the courthouse yard, back where the incinerator is, where all the rummies hang out in cold weather." He grinned without humor as I absorbed the information. While I thought, he moved to the curb and discreetly rid himself of some of his tobacco burden, then returned.

"How'd they find that out?"

"Caught a courthouse-wall bum with Ed's billfold on him. The bum claimed he found it between some bricks at the incinerator. I guess when Quinn heard about it he investigated and found some stuff—bloodstains, a button off Ed's coat, maybe some other stuff. I didn't hear everything, but I did hear as much as I'm telling you."

"You'd think all this rain would wash any traces of blood away," I said.

"I guess it didn't," he said, as if speaking from superior knowledge. "They're holding the rummy who had the billfold."

"What name?"

"The one that ain't much. Rides on a cart. Gets the others to carry him around." He snapped his fingers, searching for the name.

"George Jones—Half-a-man?"

"That's him."

Something inside me tried to find a grin in a sea of frustration. "What's he supposed to have done—induced Ed to bend over so he could whack him?"

"Does sound silly, don't it. I don't know. He had the billfold. They're telling it around that someone else might have been in it with him."

I was tempted to speculate openly that Half couldn't and wouldn't hurt anyone, but it seemed a very good time to keep the opinion to myself. But I knew Half. He drank and he was crippled. He was also bright. I thought he was much too bright to get involved in anything which could interfere with his way of life.

Gosport examined my face, reading something there, possibly remembering that Half was a friend. "Don't you make things worse than they is," he warned. "Let other stuff alone. Don't tamper. You go on doing your job and trying Amos's case."

It was very good advice and I nodded.

"Anything else going on with you?" he asked.

I thought about the telephone calls and the night intruder. I had no real proof that either was politically inspired.

"Nothing to speak of," I said. But then I told him.

"Sounds like they're trying hard to scare you off. If you

quit that would leave things to Perry Bobbin and Amos by default."

"I'm not going to do that," I said.

"I know, but they don't."

"You ever had anything like that happen to you?" I asked.

"Similar. But I'm harder to crack than you. I don't have anyone to worry about but myself. Once, a long time ago, Amos sent a couple of his best around. I had me a little advance notice." He nodded, remembering. "That was one of my better days."

"He won't try that on me," I said confidently.

"He'll try anything that ever worked for him in the past, Mickey. Amos ain't a sensitive man. He works from memory, not intelligence. You watch him."

"I will."

He looked away from me. "Got to get to work and there's no time like the present." He shook my hand once then moved away, giving up the problem he couldn't effectively deal with for one he could.

"Seven o'clock," he said, over his shoulder.

"All right," I called.

Late exiters were still leaving the church. Gosport ignored me. He spied someone he knew and moved toward him, jaws working, fierce old eyes intent, a man going to work at what he did best.

I spotted Prosecuting Attorney Allen Dunwich. He nodded and came toward me. His face was serious.

He said: "They took your policeman away."

"I wondered. I didn't see one last night. Joe Pierceton

drove past once. And someone got into the basement last night." I repeated the story once more.

"And whoever it was turned on a gas jet?" he repeated, worried about it.

I nodded. "It could have been anyone," I said. "I don't think it was Chili Blackwell because of the phone call. And no harm done."

"The mayor got jumped about police being used for your protection," he said apologetically. "Thereafter the police chief got a personal call from the mayor calling the watch off." He nodded. "I may try to make some other arrangements. But I don't know if I can." His eyes evaded mine.

"What's the problem, Al?"

"Nothing." He lifted a hand in a futile gesture. "I guess it's just that everything in this damned town has a political reason. I can't get anything done that I want to get done. Everytime I do something, say something, try to set up something, then it gets out." He gave me an angry look. "Sure, they let me catch some small potatoes, people that didn't mean much. They let us try them. Most of them are still out on appeals. Now they'll beat you and I'll bet there's damn few days of jail time spent by any of them." He looked around. "This town deserves what it gets, Judge."

"No," I said.

He laughed without humor. "You think if that bastard beats you that anything will happen in the future? He'll get rich and I'll get more frustrated." He nodded at me.

"Maybe he won't beat me."

"Maybe. I'm trying to help."

"Thanks, Allen." I turned away. "See you in the morning."

I got into the car.

"What were all the conferences about?" Mom asked.

"Just some business with Allen," I said, evading her glance. "Gosport was more than that."

She waited.

"I think I may have acquired some unexpected campaign help."

"Gosport's an able man," Mom said.

Annie said: "He's so dirty with all that tobacco. But he does keep getting himself elected."

Mom nodded sagely.

I admitted privately to myself that it was probably far too late.

6

Chess Moves

In the morning we again resumed jury selection, but not before there were some other matters.

I talked to Allen Dunwich: "I hear there's a new suspect in Ed's death," I said to him in my office.

"Not yet," he said. "I've not yet been officially informed and my office hasn't been asked to draw up any preliminary charges. They did pick up a man on a public intoxication charge and then charged him also with theft. I understand he's to go to city court this morning." He eyed me. "You interested?"

Half-a-man had been conspicuously absent when I'd arrived that morning. So had his sidekick, Samdog Cabel. I was a dollar richer.

"I'm interested. As a private citizen I'm interested. As Ed's friend and employer I'm interested. And I'm also interested as an acquaintance—no—a friend, of Half-a-man's." I shook my head. "There's no way I could ever wind up being judge in any of this."

"I'll keep you up to date on it as much as I can," he said slowly. "My guess would be that they'd try to slip him a little jail time on the PI charge if he doesn't plead guilty to the theft. That would give them a chance to question him at greater length. If he pleads innocent to the works they'll high bond him. Maybe five hundred dollars on each charge, maybe more."

"I see."

He was still watching me. "Unless maybe you'd like me to tamper in it. I can I suppose. The police and the sheriff's folks will be buzzing around the city judge telling him what they want done and he'll be listening hard. I can call him and tell him what I want done. He's as apt to do what I want done as what they want done." He smiled. "If he doesn't I have the right to dismiss. I've used it before when things got hairy and I didn't get my own way."

I hesitated. I hated the idea of the ruined little man being in jail. Although he ran with the rummies and I knew he drank I'd never seen him drunk. I thought of him on his cart, dirty gloved, the rest shining clean.

In a way I was him and he was me. Fragments.

"Let me use the phone in your office," Allen said smoothly, reading me. "I'll call down there at city court."

"No," I said. "Forget it for now. I can't ask you to do that. But I would appreciate you telling me what goes on as you find it out. As I said I'll have to disqualify myself in any of this anyhow so there'll be no long-range harm done."

"All right." He looked at me and shook his head. "I'll tell you what I think's happening now. Someone killed Ed. That's certain and we know it. The police here are normal police. They have a tendency toward cleanliness. That means that in due course someone will eventually be tried and hopefully convicted and sentenced for Ed's murder. Right now they've got themselves their first good suspect or suspects. They'll go after it like a dog after a day-old bone." He looked at me. "Would Ed and the cripple have been acquainted?"

"I'm sure they would. Probably at least from the time when Ed was sheriff, if not before that."

Allen smiled. "Maybe Ed could have been checking things out around the courthouse itself. If you listen you can hear wild stories that you can buy anything you want in front of our lovely courthouse. Not that our capable sheriff has ever caught anyone."

He stopped talking and together we watched the arrival of Amos Walker, the prisoner-accused. He came down the hall regally, dressed in a fresh suit. He was accompanied by Joe Pierceton, who walked smilingly beside him. The two men stopped down the hall and fell into an easy, low-voiced discussion about an unknown subject. Jurors-to-be wandered curiously past them.

Joe Pierceton was, as usual, impeccably uniformed. He wore a holstered gun on one side of his Sam Brown belt and a leaded night stick on the other. He was supposed to be equally good with either weapon. I wondered what had happened to him after he'd come past my house Saturday night and then remembered that he'd planned to night watch the offices.

In the times I'd had him as a witness in court I'd been impressed with his appearance and demeanor as a witness. And he was my one real contact in the sheriff's office. An easy, smiling man.

I went on into my little courtroom and took my place on the bench. The room's spectator seats were already packed. In a little while the rest of the active participants were in and ready. Amos sat in his chair. Whenever I looked his way he glared at me. His lawyer, George Higer, sat on one side of him. Several aides sat behind Higer ready to do his bidding. The uniformed Joe Pierceton sat on the other side of Amos. I could hear the distant buzzing of the prospective jurors waiting in the outer jury room to be called in.

This morning they would wait a few moments longer.

I said: "Lieutenant Pierceton, you will approach the bench. Mr. Higer and Mr. Dunwich also."

They came. Higer appeared to be mystified, but Dunwich nodded to himself and Pierceton had an expectant look.

I said: "Lieutenant Pierceton, I'm wondering whether the sheriff might have spelled out for you the way you're to guard your prisoner? It appears, at best, to be nonchalant. This might lead an onlooker or a juryman to believe that the defendant and the sheriff's department were involved together in the matter before the court. Therefore we'll lay down a few rules which you may convey to the good sheriff. First: No officer guarding Mr. Walker will sit next to him. The guard's chair will be removed from him at least ten feet, and behind him, along the wall." I pointed. "Secondly: No person guarding him will speak

to him in the presence of the jury or a jury member.
Third: He will be guarded in the normal manner."

He smiled at me boyishly. "Yes, Your Honor. I was ordered about how to guard him by the sheriff, Judge." His
eyes flicked from Higer to me and back again. "No
offense, sir, but that's how it is."

"Up here anyone the sheriff sends will take orders from
me," I said gently.

Pierceton did a very good imitation of a man caught
between two fires. He hesitated, as if unsure of his course.
With the eye that was away from Higer he gave me a
wink that was so quick I almost didn't catch it.

"I'll want to dictate a formal objection on this," Higer
said.

"Of course. And I'll be interested in seeing just how
you phrase it, Mr. Higer."

He looked me over coldly. "I believe I'll let this opportunity pass. You're within your power."

"Thank you for agreeing, Mr. Higer. You don't know
how good you make me feel." I turned to Joe Pierceton.
"And you'll pass on my words to the high sheriff in this,
Lieutenant? Tell him if he finds it disagreeable that I'll
order the defendant removed to the city lockup to be held
there and guarded by their people during the remainder
of the trial."

He hesitated. Once again I got the phantom wink, so
transitory that I wasn't sure it had happened. "The sheriff
said . . ." he began.

Higer shushed him with an imperious, upraised hand.
"He'll go along."

"You appear to have great influence in the sheriff's direction, Mr. Higer," Allen Dunwich drawled.

Higer had the grace to appear momentarily discomfited. He went to the defense table and had a few intense words with Amos.

Lieutenant Pierceton moved his chair. He sat it along the wall.

The prospective jurors were brought in by my bailiffs. The jurors were seated in the box and in vacant seats at the front of the courtroom. We were running out of prospects and I thought I might have to call the jury commissioners in to draw more names.

Voir dire began again.

I could almost physically sense that something was, on this day, different in the courtroom. Before, it had seemed to me that Higer was foot-dragging, stalling. Maybe he'd been enjoying the byplay created by the situation of the defendant and his guards. Maybe something had happened over the weekend, some decision. Now he appeared ready to move. He asked only automatic questions, he didn't fuss interminably with his papers, and he kept passing the jury back to Allen Dunwich.

I could see that this was upsetting to Dunwich, that he was puzzled and perhaps apprehensive about it, unwilling to accept the new Higer posture or the apparent gift horse that accompanied it—suspicious.

I looked over the jurors who'd been tentatively accepted. I knew or knew of most of them. Five were farmers, two were factory workers, three were housewives. There was a young, female teacher, unmarried, and a young, semi-retired engineer, male, who'd had a stroke a few months back and now was eager to serve, to do something again. They looked all right to me. A better than average jury.

Amos thought he had one or more of them in his corner. I decided that had to be it. Someplace he could trace a connection, an old debt, a political alliance. I smiled to myself. Jurors are peculiar animals. They are separate creatures, but sometimes, in the course of a lengthy trial, they become one whole creature and act that way, losing single identity in the over-all whole.

I was going to give them a good chance to do that. I'd decided that over the weekend. If someone could call me, then a juror could be called and pressured. If someone could invade my basement then a juror's home would be a vulnerable target.

In front of the bench, striding back and forth, Allen Dunwich pursued his questionings: ". . . And you will not let this presumption of innocence become a shield to protect the guilty?" he asked, pressing hard.

We were down to nods. All nodded. The twelve were ringwise. They'd heard all the questions and seen how their fellows fielded them, learned from those answers. They knew the desired response.

Allen moved on, attacking the jury with questions as a whole, then going after its members singly. Had they ever been involved as a party or witness in a trial? Had they ever had a bad experience with a peace or police officer? Were they friendly with anyone now involved in the party run by Amos? Some admitted to the last, but further questions got negative head shakes, smiles, grunts. It was an attack without success. If there was someone on the jury who was tinged with ownership by Amos Walker, nothing showed on the surface.

After a long time probing, Allen Dunwich turned to me, raised one eyebrow slightly in defeat, and said: "The state accepts the jury, Your Honor."

By noon we had not only a jury, but two alternates, sworn, ready to go. Now they were creatures of the state. Smiling bailiffs took them to lunch.

I sent Jen down the street for her lunch and asked her to bring back a sandwich for me. Work time. I spent the noon hour going over the routine preliminary instructions: Credibility, burden of proof, presumption of innocence, and the like.

Jen returned after a while with my cheeseburger. "The town's stirring around out there. Everyone seems to know there's a jury. The people in the next booth were arguing about whether or not Amos Walker is guilty." She shook her head. "The vote was one for guilty, three for acquittal, and two thought you'd get killed while the trial was going on."

"Let's hope it isn't that bad," I said. "They've been reading the local newspaper. Amos owns a big chunk of it. He's had good press. Hopefully, since we've warned the prospective jurors about reading on the case, they haven't been reading it. And besides what they see and hear now should overrule what the paper says. And we'll also make it impossible for the jury to read about it during the trial." I looked up at her. "What's the most private hotel-motel in town?"

"Queen's Motel," she said without hesitation. "They

run it like a sanitarium. No TV, no room telephones, no radio."

"Call them. Make the arrangements. Our jury won't go home for a few nights."

"Fourteen rooms or seven?"

"Seven rooms." A witness in every room in case anything was attempted. "Plus one more for one of the special bailiffs." I nodded. "I want the other one to go to my house and be there during the day. I want him armed."

"Use Coulson," she said. "He likes guns."

"Coulson, then," I said, trying to remember which one he was.

"I'll tell him to go to the house," she said. "You want him to start today?"

I nodded. "I think so. He can go to the house every day while this trial's on."

"How long do you think the trial will last?"

"A week maybe. Could be longer."

"Then it could be done by primary election day?"

"I don't know. Possibly."

"You won't have much time to campaign," she said.

"I'll do what I can at nights. Tonight I'm supposed to go with Gosport to a meeting—a party thing. He thinks we might make some real inroads."

"Your opponent doesn't even miss an auction," she said. "I think if someone was building a garage that Perry would be there to make the dedication speech."

"That's right," I said noncommittally.

"He's pretty," she added. "All those white teeth and his little bow tie. He was in here the other day and told me I could stay on if I could square things with Amos Walker."

"That's interesting."

She tossed her head, disgusted at not being able to draw me into some kind of argument. But I didn't feel like arguing.

The telephone rang and she grabbed it.

"Judge Tostini's office."

She listened for a moment. "Hold for a minute," she said. She pushed down her hold button and looked at me and then the phone.

"It's Randy Rumple. Do you want to talk to him?"

I nodded and took the phone.

"Hello, Randy."

He got right to the point: "How about meeting me for a drink and some conversation at the country club when day is done, friend Judge?"

"It'll have to be a short one," I said, remembering that Gosport was coming past for our foray into enemy territory.

"Five o'clock like?"

"All right." There would be time. I'd make time. Randy was part of the party machinery. Maybe he wanted to tell me something of use.

———◆———

That afternoon I read preliminary instructions and counsel made predictable opening statements. Allen Dunwich seemed to be getting some mileage out of the viciousness of the crime, the number of blows struck. He talked about his star witness not being there because she was the victim of the crime.

Higer merely asked the jury to make certain that the

state proved its case against the defendant and was cold and contemptuous of its ability to do so. His *voir dire* questioning had been heavy on what could be believed from circumstantial evidence.

When Higer finished and clumped to his seat it was after four o'clock. I called a halt to it for the day. Tomorrow the state would begin presentation of its case.

I went into my office and put my feet up. They'd started emptying the wastebaskets only sporadically again and someone had gotten the books on my bookshelves badly out of order.

In a little while Allen Dunwich came to the door and I motioned him on in.

"I checked with a policeman who came by to see what was happening. The gentleman you asked about earlier today entered a plea of not guilty to charges of theft and public intoxication." He grinned. "The policeman said that he was carried into city hall and back out again, completely unco-operative. He said he'd heard the only thing they've gotten out of him so far was the plea and his name. I guess they hassled around at city court on the bond. Maybe the sheriff's people got to thinking about all the work of having a cripple as a prisoner. Anyway, they finally agreed on a total bond of five hundred dollars."

"Thanks for the information," I said.

"He can buy himself a bond and get out by paying a bondsman 10 per cent, fifty dollars," Allen explained.

"I know."

Jen came to the door and Allen bounced to his feet and on to the door.

"See you in the morning," he promised, and closed the door.

"I'll drive you home," I said to Jen. "I've got to meet Randy at five and then I've got a meeting at seven with Gosport. Okay if I come past for you thereafter?"

"You'd better had," she said, smiling with mock severity.

In a while we moved out, locking doors behind us. We took the elevator down. Downstairs the halls were deserted. The jury had been escorted to their motel. Higer and Amos had conferred furiously about that.

In front of the courthouse there was some minor activity. Samdog Cabel stood stiffly out there in the yard, his back to a tree trunk. A few pedestrians looked him over curiously. The courthouse wall was deserted for the early evening wine-sharing hour.

Samdog held a sign up high, waving it slowly. It was light enough for me to see it well. It read, in crudely printed letters: FREE HALF.

I could have gone out the back way, but I decided against it. I clutched Jen's arm and went boldly out the front door. Samdog spied me.

He was clean for once. Someone had given him a needed bath and put him in a ragged, but immaculate shirt. His hair was pushed back away from his slightly off-focus eyes. I thought the greater need of rescuing Half from jail might even have temporarily sobered him.

He eyed Jen and shuffled his feet. "The world's a prostitute," he said apologetically.

"How much have you put together to get Half a bond?" I asked.

"I got thirty dollars," he said rationally. "I got thirty out of them wall guys." He looked out at the deserted area and I knew why they'd fled earlier. "Who'd have believed they'd have thirty dollars or that I could get it out of them?" He shook his head.

I got out my semi-limp billfold and gave him twenty dollars.

He eyed the bill in disbelief.

"You ain't a real bad son of a bitch," he said. "I mean what with you being a judge."

———◆▶———

I dropped Jen off and then drove on to the country club. I parked the Monte Carlo in a parking lot crowded with a mixture of cars. About half the vehicles were luxury cars, Cadillacs, Lincolns, Chryslers, huge paneled station wagons, and the like. But the rest were Audis, Toyotas, Datsuns, and American copies of the same. Changing times.

I don't belong to the country club. Somehow I've managed to survive. There was a time when I was often invited there, but those invitations, once I'd fallen out of favor with the party, had died away.

I went on through the swinging glass doors and spied Randy in the bar. He was in the middle of making a point to a polite, black bartender. He stopped when he saw me.

"Hi, Judge," he said. "Would you take a drink?"

I considered it and then nodded.

"Martini on the rocks," I said.

Randy nodded approvingly. I didn't remember seeing his vehicle in the lot. Randy's wife owns a big farm and

Randy, in addition to being a sometime lawyer, is a gentleman farmer. He drives one of those low-slung trucks which look more like race cars than utility vehicles and which would probably die of shame if a bale of hay was placed in their truck bed.

He waited until the bartender slid him my drink. He handed it to me grandly and surveyed the large, semi-dark room on the far side of the bar. Inside it a fire burned fitfully in a fireplace and waitresses moved about quickly, as if getting ready for the peak of the evening.

"Let's go in there," he said.

"All right."

I followed him to a secluded table. Most of the room was empty, but there were a few early diners and a few early drinkers. From another room I could hear the sounds of piano music, laughter, and voices raised in song.

Randy sat me down and smiled at me and I reflected that we'd known each other most of our lives. He was later out of law school than I was. I'd gone and then entered service and he'd entered service and then gone, but we were the same age. In high school we'd dated the same girls, in undergraduate school we'd once roomed together before he'd gone on to his fraternity house. Despite those early times together we'd never been good friends, but only close acquaintances, driven to room together that one time by necessity, dating the same girls because there was no other available product.

Randy was a bright enough lawyer, even if he was more of a planner than a doer. I had mixed feelings about him. It was hard to think of him as an enemy when there were all those years behind us. I thought it was probably

Randy who'd arranged Higer's defense of Amos, but that was all right. It didn't make any difference to me whether Amos was convicted or not. My job was to give him a fair trial. I also figured that Randy had been consulted about every member of the jury. Randy was a man who shunned the spotlight but loved smoke-filled rooms and intrigue. He lived in dread of loss, but he could also bring winning along with him by his very hatred of losing. He had a bright-penny wife who owned the huge farm and had lots of family money and who pushed him mercilessly.

When I'd gone on the bench he'd renewed our old relationship by inviting me to parties, by including me. In a small town it had been something to do. So we had become "friends" again, but of course lately the relationship had disintegrated.

Now I waited curiously.

He tinkled the ice in his Beefeater's idly.

"I wanted to talk to you before it was too late," he said. "You're getting yourself deeper and deeper into a cess-pool. You can put a stink on yourself that will last and stay with you the rest of your years here."

"Horse manure, Randy. I'm one of the functionaries in a trial. I didn't commit the crime, make the arrest, return the indictment, or decide to prosecute it. And I'm getting a little tired of being viewed and spoken of as some sort of a mastermind out to 'get' Amos Walker. I think he knows and you know that it isn't so." I smiled at him, pushing him a little. "I expect people who are friends of mine to stick up for me and explain that."

I saw his lip curl a little, a reaction he'd never been

able to control fully when we were kids. I wasn't to be allowed to presume upon friendship. That was his privilege alone.

He said carefully: "The best thing you could do for yourself would be to withdraw from the judge's race."

"I wonder why?" I asked. "So it can be easy? I don't believe I'm going to do that. I like the job. And in trying Amos, after he and whoever is advising him gave me no choice, I feel like I'm doing what has to be done. So I won't quit."

I saw him look around. This was his territory. He wanted no scenes. My voice had gone up and he was nervous about that, but no one seemed to be looking.

"Who asked you to try with me, Randy?"

"Party people," he said stoutly. "A lot of them. Some of them used to be your friends." He looked me over, distaste not far back in his eyes. Amos was in trouble and Randy was high in the machinery of the party. Someone had said to leave me on the bench. Someone had told them I'd do their bidding. Now I was in the way. He calculated his chances again as he watched me and liked those chances.

"You told them to keep me on the bench, didn't you, Randy?" I asked softly.

He was still calculating, remembering girls won, remembering athletic contests, grades in classes, forgetting all the times I'd won and remembering only his own victories.

"What?" he asked.

"Nothing, I guess."

"I wish you'd withdraw, Mickey. It would be better for

all of us. If you lose, it might be very hard for you to do business in this town with both judges angry at you."

"You ever heard about a motion for a change of venue from the judge, Randy?"

"That's all right for some things, but a lot of the business has to be done in front of our local judges—estate stuff—routine things, bread and butter."

"If I lost and things began to become difficult for me I just might scream very loudly in places where such screams might echo a little. And I might save those screams and the documentation for them for opportune and painful times—like near elections."

"Why don't you just go over and join the other party?" he asked, voice reasonable.

"Why don't you instead, Randy?" I said, smiling. I wasn't really angry, but I was getting there.

"No one wants me to . . ." he began, and then stopped.

"I do. I just said it. And I'm a candidate for high office." I kept smiling.

"Let's not be unpleasant," he said.

I leaned a little toward him. "What happened, Randy? Was there another little backroom meeting. Did you tell them you were sorry it hadn't worked so far, but you still knew old Mickey *real* well and you thought you could at least talk him into dropping out?"

His face changed just enough.

"I was thinking about you, Mickey. I was worried about you."

I was weary of the whole scene. I was tired of people who wanted me out for all the wrong reasons, who thought I was going to be beaten for all the wrong rea-

sons. I was sick of it. I remembered the veiled offers I'd
had and I remembered the open and available offers I'd
had. I was frustrated by all of it and he was the only
thing within immediate reach.

I said: "Go back and tell them it didn't work, Randy.
Tell them to take the judgeship if they can. And tell
them the next one they send along to try and make anything happen is going to get more than his nose rubbed in
it."

He stuck his jaw out pugnaciously. "We'll beat you,
Mickey."

"Probably." He watched me as I stood up and I recalled a line out of an old joke. The room had filled some
and people were looking at us, but it was his club, not
mine. And I knew his copper-haired wife was insanely
jealous and not without reason.

I said, in a loud voice: "Thanks for the drinks, friend
Randy, but tell the girls you hired for later that I couldn't
make it." I patted his shoulder. "You take care of them."

I saw his face redden and a nearby woman gasped.

I turned away and went out the glass door and into the
parking lot. What I'd done was small and childish and
mean.

I felt good about it.

7

Political Meeting

Later that evening, ready a little early and nervous at the
thought of invading the territory of the enemy, I stood on
the front lawn of the old house. Behind me the turretlike
roof that covered the steps up to the house was lit by one
weak light bulb. Up the street three children played lack-
adaisical stoop tag in the growing gloom. The neighborhood had changed. When I'd grown up in it there had
been many kids. Now, most of the residents were old and
the only children were occasional grandchildren visiting
the old folks, children who eyed the big old trees with
awe and ill-concealed desire to conquer, children who
yelled carefully. The quiet of the neighborhood was not
complete compensation.

Gosport pulled up in his old car and tooted the horn,
bringing me up from my memories. I saw Mom pull back
a curtain and peep out, then let it slide quickly back,

afraid of being seen. Anna had gone on to the college library, escorted by a car full of laughing boys and girls. The bailiff, Coulson, had gone home when I'd gotten in from the country club.

I got in the front seat with Gosport. He grinned at me. "Just stay close to me," he advised. "I know the weak spots. Follow my cues when you can."

"Sure," I said. "Who'll be running the meeting with Amos in jail?"

"Probably Sheriff Zisk and maybe Randy Rumple helping," he said.

"That should be interesting." I described my meeting earlier in the evening with Randy.

"They'd never have come after you to try to get you out if they were sure," he said, nodding. "They's just a hell of a lot of people not saying anything. If they thought they was going to get them people they'd not want you out—they'd want to rub your nose in it." He shook his head. "Who knows what a voter will do on election day."

We drove sedately to headquarters. It was located in an old building on the edge of town. Once it had been a small factory. The party had bought it in bad times, paid it off in good, and neglected it down all the years. The roof leaked and the window frames were rotting. The inside was dirty and the outside needed paint. The main decorations on the walls were pictures of deceased politicians who'd once held high office.

There were plenty of parking spaces and plenty of room inside the drafty interior of the building.

We parked and walked up. A few people smiled at me,

friends that I'd almost forgotten I had. A few other people did double takes when they saw me with Gosport. Once inside we melted into the crowd with Gosport introducing me to the several I didn't know, spotting possibles here and there in the crowd, dragging me on. I kept smiling and shaking hands.

A party organization is a hodgepodge of people. If I knew the organization, it accepted Amos Walker and kept re-electing him because he won elections and because they hated those who wanted to take over from him worse than they hated Amos.

"I knew your father," an old lady said. She held my hand tightly and looked in my eyes, wanting as much contact as possible.

"I guess a judge has to do what's legal," a farmer told me stolidly, his eyes steadily on my face. "If old Gosport here says you're all right, then you're all right with me." He shook his head. "Although we sure have gotten a lot of talk."

"Don't you think women should take a major part in politics?" asked a sharp-nosed young lady with steel-rimmed spectacles. She was no-bra and needed the help of one badly.

"What's your opinion as to what the drinking age should be, Judge?" a thin young man asked, his blue eyes intent and interested.

"I'm a party man most times," a middle-aged ward captain said in a low voice, "but I don't like being told what to do in a primary—threatened even. You stick with Gosport, Judge. You'll do all right." He winked. "I'll help."

I smiled and shook hands, shook hands and smiled. Moved on.

Up front I saw Sheriff Hen Zisk conferring with Randy Rumple. They were watching me. The sheriff went to the microphone. He rang a hand bell loudly for attention. Randy stood beside him, smiling at the audience.

I'd met Zisk's opponent in my meanderings with Gosport. His name was Trent McGuire and I'd liked him. He'd seemed sober enough to me, although I'd heard (from Zisk?) that he was a semi-reformed alcoholic. I knew one vote that Mr. McGuire would get.

My heart was gladdened when Gosport whispered: "Don't count on nothin' for Hen. They's just one hell of a bunch of folks that have had it to the nose with him. You listen around." He grinned. "But Hen don't know it."

"You mean that Hen might get beat?" I asked, delighted.

"Maybe."

Up front, Randy Rumple began to call the roll, introducing all. He started at the township level, asking advisory board candidates to rise, then he went on to township trustees. When he got to the courthouse aspirants he asked each candidate if he desired to say anything to the crowd in fifteen seconds or less. Most shuffled their feet and grinned and let him go on. They had no opposition.

Hen Zisk's opponent stood up, seemed to consider making a speech, and then quite obviously decided against facing Hen at the microphone. He smiled and raised a hand. There was a good round of applause and some open cheering, while Hen frowned as he stood beside Randy Rumple.

All of the candidate introductions and occasional short speeches by those candidates had taken some time. It seemed to me that the crowd was becoming restless. In the back of the room I saw one reason. There were two half barrels of beer back there. The barrels sat in their containers, iced and ready.

I'd lost Gosport and stood by myself. Around me people ebbed and flowed. Some of them nodded and spoke, but some went past me as if I wasn't there.

My opponent, Perry L. Bobbin, went eagerly up to the front when he was introduced. He shuffled his way through the crowd, shaking a hand here, clapping a shoulder there. He was wearing his best and he shone brightly. His bow tie bobbed a little, following his Adam's apple. He took the microphone from the unprotesting Randy Rumple.

"Friends," he said. "All my friends. I'm happy to be here with you tonight. My only regret is that our good leader can't be here with us."

There was a little murmur in the crowd and Perry continued on: "I talked with him today and he told me that he'd soon be back with us. Now, I want to ask you all again for your votes and your support. You can be assured that if I'm nominated and elected I'll always remember, *that's always remember*, who elected me and not forget my friends." He smiled out in my direction and gave the mike back to Randy Rumple.

"There's beer," Hen called out to Randy.

I'd not seen Gosport near them, but suddenly he was up close and he leaped on the stage.

"You've forgotten one candidate," he said loudly, not

needing the microphone. "There's another candidate for circuit court judge that you seem to have forgotten, Randy."

Randy gave him a disdainful look. The crowd had quieted expectantly.

I moved forward quickly. In a moment the chance would be gone. Gosport took the mike from Randy's unresisting hand and passed it to me.

"Thank you for your courtesy, Randy," I said. I heard a little titter of laughter run through the crowd. "My name's Mickey Tostini and most of you know me and knew my father before me. I also know you—or most of you. I want you to know that if you are indicted or charged in my court I will still know you and will hope you know me. But that must be all there is to it. I will be fair to you and I hope you'll be fair to me. That's what this judge business is supposed to be about. And, of course, I'd like to have your support and help."

I handed the microphone back to Randy. Gosport was grinning at me. There was some applause, a ripple of it that grew. There wasn't a lot of it, but not just a little either.

The crowd was turning to the rear of the room.

"Beer?" Gosport asked.

"Just one to be polite."

He nodded, obviously pleased with me. We went back toward the rear of the room. Lieutenant Joe Pierceton, of the county police, was handling the chore of opening the first keg. He was out of uniform and looked smaller, slighter than normal. He smiled gently at me and splashed beer in a cup. I followed Gosport into the press of the crowd.

Near the front of the room I spied Sheriff Hen Zisk in deep conversation with several of his cronies, hangers-on at the sheriff's office. Gosport was also watching them.

"Time to move on," he said to me. "Those boys are the storm troopers. They'll do anything Hen tells them to do. We stick around and there'll be an incident. We did too well here for us to take any chances on such an incident."

We hastened toward a side door. There I shook one last hand and was through, out into the night. Around us non-drinkers hastened toward their cars.

"You did just fine," Gosport said. "I was proud of you. You knew not to make a speech, but you got the needle in good."

"Thanks," I said.

"You'd be surprised how many politicians live their whole lives out without ever having the gift of timing."

"I just gave them the truth," I said.

"And you'd also be surprised how many people never believe in any of the truth," he said.

We got into his old Chevvie. He fired it up and said: "Lock your door."

I nodded and pushed down the button. We chugged between lanes of cars out toward the street. Something rattled off the hood of the car and starred the windshield on my side. There was a great, banging sound. I didn't see what it was, but Gosport pressed down on the accelerator and we shot out of the lot.

"A rock," he said.

In the street we watched behind us, but there was no

immediate sign of pursuit. Gosport pulled a plug of tobacco out of his pocket, breathed deeply, and bit himself
off a piece. He offered it and when I declined he rolled
down his window.

"Thank you for taking me," I said.

He smiled. "I was happy to do it. Your daddy did me
some turns when he was about your age. Maybe helping
you is a kind of repayment."

"What did he do?" I asked curiously.

He shook his head. "I disremember. Maybe it was just
telling me things. Long as I can remember people have
liked to tell me things. They tell me something, then I tell
them something. I got a friend in the sheriff's office who
passes me on things and I tell him things in exchange. I
heard in there that your crippled friend is out. I don't
think they'll pick him up again without a whole bunch of
evidence. Too crazy for even Hen Zisk." His lip curled a
little.

"Joe Pierceton tell you that?"

"What?" he asked, although I was sure he'd heard me.

"You say you've got a friend in the sheriff's office. Is it
Lieutenant Joe Pierceton?"

He looked at me and waited.

"Reason I ask is that he's about the only one there
who's been all right with me."

He nodded. "I won't deny or admit he's the one. But I
will say that he's a pretty good man. Someday, if he plays
the deck right, he may wind up being sheriff."

"I'd vote that way."

"You see how Randy and Hen ran the meeting?" He
shook his head. "They learned from a good teacher, Amos

Walker. Don't operate for fair. Just bulldoze straight ahead. You got any friends who get into this drug business with you you tell them to look over Hen and Randy real good. Until he went to jail the rumor was that Amos was getting a top cut off the drug money. Maybe he wasn't running it alone, but he was big in it. Someone's had to take over his place. My bet is that good old Hen is the top local now. Randy ain't, because he don't need the money bad enough. Old Hen's kissing at Amos and treating him nice and keeping things in line for him. Plus getting a good lick off the top. Hen always did have the morals of a semi-retired prostitute."

"I thought you told me once you weren't against Hen?" I said, grinning.

"That was before the last few days. Now I think he might be beatable."

We drove on in silence and he finally stopped the car in front of my house. Mom had turned the outside lights on, a precaution we'd agreed on, but which her economical heart frowned on. No police vehicle seemed to be in attendance upon the house.

"Tomorrow the stores stay open until nine at night," Gosport advised. "When your trial's done for the day I want you to wander around your town. You will smile at everyone, hear? You'll go in the stores and buy a few things. Buy one thing one place, another thing in another place. I want at least a hundred people to see you!"

"Yes, boss," I said humbly.

He nodded fiercely and drove away.

I waited until he was out of sight and then went into the house, using my key to open the door. Mom was still awake. She sat in her wheel chair mesmerized by a televi-

sion play about doctors and hospitals and hideous dis-
eases. She nodded distractedly at me when I stood in front
of her and jingled the car keys.

"Going over to Jen's place for a little while," I said.

She nodded. Upstairs a bright light came from Anna's
room.

I went back out the front door and made certain it was
locked behind me. I looked up and down the street.
Nothing.

The Monte Carlo was in the drive. I unlocked it and
drove to Jen's apartment.

She lived in an apartment complex, three square blocks
of two-story apartments, Bedford stone outside, shag carpet halls, paint that was already starting to peel, and
musty smells inside. The apartments were fairly new, but
it seemed to me that we'd lost the knack of building first-
class, long-lived multi-units any more. We cut costs with
plastics and ersatz and somehow the whole didn't add up
to its parts. Someday, maybe soon, I thought the last wars
would be fought from inside jerry-built apartments, a few
defenders doggedly watching their televisions while the
darkness fell.

I tapped on Jen's door and she let me in. She was wearing a pants suit and she fit inside it very well, but her legs
are too good for her to wear one often without complaint
from me. We grappled cozily for a moment and then
moved on into the tiny living room. The shag inside was a
different color from the shag in the halls. From a TV in
the corner Mom's same doctors performed their miracles,
loved the patients, loved each other. Jen switched them
off.

"How'd it go?" she asked.

"All right. Real good in fact." I looked into her eyes. They were gray in the light of the single lamp. I admired her non-doll face, strictly for adults. It was a strong face and not a child's face. And I reflected that too many times we love faces and forms and not the people who inhabit them.

"Guess at your chances for me?" she ordered.

"I'm maybe the very worst person you could ask to do that," I said. I looked at her and she waited. "All right. I'd say my chances are slim. I have no organization. They do. If we have our usual, apathetic primary, then I'll get beat pretty good. The local newspaper will crow some about it and take credit. Amos Walker will give me a smug look. Then the world will go on. Winning or losing the election isn't really the thing—at least for me. I'm not going to let it hurt me." I thought a little bit more, trying to find words. "I hope I win, but I can lose without it ruining me. Maybe I'd be better off now if I did lose. You make money in the legal profession just by time spent. I've been here longer than before and my name's better known. Maybe, if I get beat, it will be easier to make a living."

"You don't really believe that," she said solemnly.

She was partially right, but I smiled. "Let's discuss it at greater length. Come closer."

She smiled in return and did just that . . .

———◄◆►———

In the morning the actual trial began. The prosecution called its first witnesses. The very first one was the coroner.

The coroner was a pudgy, little man who'd found his medical niche in life after a long search. I knew him pretty well and we were friendly. He kept a small practice in an office that adjoined his home and sent all his patients to specialists for anything more complicated than a hangnail. He charged high for such advice. But he was a nice guy and considered to be a three-martini man among his brothers at the Elks Club.

On this day he'd dressed in a sharp, checked leisure suit. He took the oath and Allen Dunwich, the prosecutor, after qualifying him, spent some time getting to the heart of the matter.

"How old was the decedent, Janet Walker?"

"Objection," Higer said.

"If you know the age of the decedent you may answer, Doctor," I said. "If someone told you her age, then you may not."

He smiled up at me, perfectly willing to put up with all this legal rigamarole. "I know."

"Then the objection is overruled. You may answer the question."

"She was thirty years old."

"Describe her physical characteristics."

"Well, she was five foot six inches tall and weighed one hundred twenty-two pounds. Well nourished, well developed." He shook his head. "Old appendectomy scar. Some fresh scratches on her back, in addition to the injuries she died of."

"What sort of scratches?"

"Just—scratches," he said hesitating. "Maybe nail scratches."

Involuntarily, with the jury, I looked down at Amos

Walker's hands. His nails were long and appeared to be sharp.

We went on in that vein for a little while, but finally got to the point.

"You're testifying then that Janet Walker died as the result of being struck repeated blows to the head with a blunt instrument?"

"Yes."

"How many blows?"

"I counted more than twenty marks. There may have been other blows which left no marks."

"Would you say her beating was savage?"

"Objection," Higer said laconically, just letting Dunwich know he was there.

"Sustained," I said before he could explain and qualify the objection. Sometimes, in order to make a record for appeal, defense counsel will hedge around the edges of reasons for his objection, use time for half speeches to the jury, and finally get at it.

Higer gave me a quick, combative look and then sat down.

"In your opinion, Doctor, *where* did Janet Walker die?"

"At her home here in Rivertown."

"What state and county?"

The good doctor told him. Venue had now been at least partially established.

Allen Dunwich retired to his table.

"Your witness," he said to Higer. "You may ask."

Higer blinked. He hadn't been hurt and he knew it. Some photos of the body and the residence had been marked and identified, but not yet offered into evidence. I waited, thinking I knew what was going through Higer's mind. He could get hurt worse if he tried to shake a confident witness. Sometimes not asking is the hardest thing an attorney can do.

"No questions," he said. I invisibly approved his decision.

The day got more hotly contested as the various investigatory officials continued to take the witness stand and testify.

The state had a fair circumstantial case against Amos. No one had seen him kill his wife, but then those who kill seldom invite audiences. And so one way to fight a massed evidence circumstantial case was to fall on every variance. This Higer did with vigor. He nitpicked very well, but I saw that the jury was, at times, restive during his slow cross examinations, seemingly not interested in what color the sky was, or whether the time was eight or five after eight, or whether the temperature was forty or thirty-nine. The problems with a defesne that builds upon variance is that sometimes unanswered major questions are lost in the mass of verbiage.

But I could tell Amos approved. Now and then his little pig eyes would glint when his counsel made some point which Amos believed was a telling one. Defendants sometimes become so enraptured in the mystique of their own cases that they begin to believe that each little area of doubt is enough to make major doubt.

I knew that the state's case, at least for the first few days of the trial, would consist mostly of city police officers who'd been routinely involved in the investigation of the homicide, officers who'd collected the evidence, taken the pictures, and thereafter been charged with custody of those items. Prosecutor Allen Dunwich had drilled them well. They sat carefully on the witness stand, each of them serious-faced, polite, co-operative. Yes, they had talked with Allen about the crime and gone over their evidence with him, but he had only told them to tell the exact truth. Tight-faced, they identified the items of clothing found in the house and on the deceased, clothes that were spotted and flooded with the dried brown stains of blood.

Accurately, the scene of the crime was painted. A modern, expensive home. Booze in the cabinets, a bottle of Bourbon on the sink. A telephone torn from the wall.

As the first day wore on Amos began to sink a little in his chair, to lose interest, as the jurors passed a bloody coat with Amos's initials down the line, their eyes shifting from the coat to Amos, then back again to the blood on the coat.

"And where did you discover the coat, Officer?"

"Well, down in the basement of the house, sir. It was behind the gas furnace."

"You say it was behind the furnace? You mean it was burned in some way?" Allen asked, fumbling deadpan with the coat as if looking for a burned area.

"No, sir. There's no good way to burn things in a gas furnace like the one in that house."

"Objection," Higer said. "Move to strike the last part of the answer as unresponsive to the question asked by the prosecutor."

I nodded to Jen. "It may go out."

Allen Dunwich smiled at me as I ordered the striking. Then he proved the situation by direct questions.

It was, at the end of the first day of trial, at least a day of minor triumphs for the prosecution. I could look at Higer and sense in him that he now knew his client could be convicted, that the prosecutor was competent, even smart. Some aren't. Higer and Amos could look forward to some long days of the same sort of thing while the mass of evidence became heavy enough to sink Amos.

I adjourned at a little before five.

8

Foray

At dinner Annie gave me a piece of notepaper. Two names and one address were written on it.

"Those are the names you were interested in—the boys Ed was talking to when I saw him."

"Any trouble getting it?" I asked anxiously.

She shook her head and smiled. "I just asked a boy I know and he knew their names."

"Thanks, little sister," I said. I shoved the note in my pocket and went back at dinner. Mom watched suspiciously, saying nothing.

The address was a faded brick building near the university. The street outside was potholed. Downstairs in the building was a cut-rate druggist and a quick pizza place. The neighborhood was mixed, mostly kids, and seemed relaxed, almost happy. But I had Jen lock the car

doors while I entered the dark side stairs and went up to
the second floor. There were three apartments up there.
Two of them had door name cards which meant nothing.
The third door was blank.

I knocked carefully on the third door. A voice called
out an unintelligible something behind the door and I
waited for a time and then knocked again more loudly.

A bearded boy opened the door a crack and then
wider. He was thin to the point of emaciation. He wore
no shirt although the air which came from the apartment
seemed cool. He grinned amiably at me.

"I know you from somewhere," he said, shaking his
head and trying to make memory come.

"I'm a friend of Ed Long's."

"No. Ed doesn't have any friends now. He's dead." He
bowed his head a little, seemingly sorry about it.

"I want to talk to you about him," I said.

"All right." He opened the door all the way and let me
squeeze past him.

The apartment was a jackdaw land of used kitchen-
ware, plates, cups, glasses, piled high on various tables
and in the kitchen alcove that made up one corner of the
central room. There was an old couch with bright, soiled
pillows. Magazines and books were piled here and there
around the floor and against the walls. Everything was
dusty, dingy. A single, uncurtained window of wavy glass
gave an imperfect view of the street outside.

He motioned me to a rickety chair and I sat in it carefully.

"You ain't selling anything?" he asked.

"No. Are you Rick Vidan?"

He shook his head, suddenly wary of me.

"Then you must be Pete Manning."

"All right," he admitted. "What about Ed and why did you come to see me and Rick?"

"Ed Long worked for me," I said. I added a lie: "He had your names and the address of this place in his confidential files."

"Ed didn't work for anyone, mister," he argued with a little life in his voice. "He did what he did on his own."

"He was my bailiff part time."

He nodded, accepting that for the moment. "He did say something a few times about working for a judge. You ain't very old to be a judge," he finished doubtfully. "If you'd let your hair grow and get you a beard you could live around here."

"Why was Ed talking to you and Rick a few days back?"

He shrugged. "I don't remember. We talked with Ed lots of times."

I said: "Someone killed him not long after he last talked to you."

He nodded and I could see some feeling in his eyes. "I know. I read it in a paper. But me'n Rick don't know nothing about it. Ed was always asking us about what we heard from across the river. He didn't care about this sinkhole over here." He shook his head. "He was a good guy."

I nodded. "Did you tell him anything about something going on across the river?"

"Not really. Nothing he didn't know. There's a lot of rumors going around about a big shipment coming in. We didn't know where, we didn't know when. And what we told Ed wasn't new to him. Understand?"

"No," I said. But it did mean that he had been investigating drugs.

"Ed turned me and Rick loose once—a year or two back —when we were kids." He gave me a look in which fear was mixed with guilt. "We called him and he came over and we told him what was going around. Rick's scared and so am I. Maybe someone saw Ed with us and killed him because of that. And maybe that someone figures we might give out with more. It could be very bad."

"What did Ed say when you told him?"

"He said he'd heard about it from several sources. He said something about it maybe being watered stock soon."

"Watered stock?"

"That's what he said. And then he laughed and bought us our Cokes and told us not to worry."

I looked around the apartment. "Where's Rick?"

"At school now." He shook his head. "Ed scared us when he caught us. We don't mess around with anything hard—not even at parties. Smoke a little grass is all. Rick don't hardly even do that. He wants to get into law school."

I nodded. Their world was not my world. I was ten plus years older. Drugs had been present when I grew up, but not the way they were now. The drug world has become an intricate thing, complex and slippery. The levels in it are no longer sharply discernible—except at the top. Somehow the battle's been lost. Law won all the skirmishes, but lost anyway.

Ed had a propensity for taking things into his own hands. An aging knight errant.

I said good-by to the boy and he let me out into the hall thankfully. I went down the dirty stairs.

———◆———

Outside I sat in the car without starting it for a long time, just thinking. Jen watched me, her eyes green in the lights from the neon of the drugstore and pizza parlor.

"What is it?" she asked.

"Someone is or was bringing in shipments of drugs over and around our fair city. Ed knew about it. So he went up around the courthouse to watch or wait or tell someone. And he got himself killed."

"You think maybe the drugs were being delivered around the courthouse—is that it?"

"I don't know. But I think I've got a good idea of where they're bringing the drugs in—or at least where they were bringing them in."

She gave me a questioning look.

"On the river, Jen. Someone's bringing them in by boat, probably by pleasure cruiser or maybe an innocuous-appearing houseboat. And you can bet they're coming upriver from New Orleans by towboat, aboard a load of oil or foreign cars maybe." I nodded to myself. "Ed said something to those kids. He called it watered stock." Something else flickered in my head, right behind my eyes. "Maybe watered stock meant a little more than just on the river."

She looked at me. "Now's the time to go see that police lieutenant and tell him about it and let him handle it."

"You're right. I'm going to tell Tiny Quinn—and soon. I

think he's probably all right. I'm not sure, but I'm not sure of much these days. I'll tell the prosecutor, too. But maybe not just yet."

"Why wait?"

I shrugged. "Somehow things that get told get to be public property awfully quick around our town, Jen. I tell Tiny, then he has to make up a report. Other people see it. I tell the prosecutor, then he has to do something about it. He's not a police officer. That means he has to tell the state boys maybe. Suddenly there's lots of people around, all falling over each other, obscuring things, creating a fog. And in the fog I don't know who's on my side."

She faced me, her eyes serious. "I think you ought to tell someone and get out of it."

"You're probably right."

"But you're not going to do it that way—are you?"

"Not yet—it isn't ready to be told yet."

"What are you going to do until you do decide to tell someone?"

I smiled at her. I knew something I was going to do later, but I decided it wasn't right to get her involved in it.

I said: "Right now I'm going to drive back across the river and feed you something and then we're going to walk through the downtown section with frequent stops, making some purchases. That's on the advice of my expert campaign chairman, Gosport McFay. Then I'm going to take you home." I looked out into the darkness. "I want to get home fairly early. I need to give things a good think through."

"Take me home with you and I'll help you think," she said, smiling.

"No. Not tonight. I take you home and Mom thinks it's party time." I remembered the intruder in the basement. That could have been a party too.

We drove on across the river. I could see she was lost in thought. I'd given her an anchor when things had gone bad—given her a job she liked and in the area she wanted to work in. Now that might soon vanish.

I fed her a cheeseburger and fries at a neoned drive-in inhabited by brightly garbed kids who chattered and car-hopped gaily.

For a short time we wandered sedately through the downtown section of my town. I bought a new pair of shoes, three ties, some handkerchiefs, socks. She bought junk jewelry and a bright scarf. Store operators greeted us cautiously. I thought they were aware of what I was doing, but they were willing to be conned along. In most places I was introduced to the help. Two store owners claimed privately and bitterly to me in undertones that Perry L. Bobbin "bought across the river," at least a venial sin.

I had a feeling that things were bubbling hard and I wanted to be on with it. I called Mom once and all was well, but I cut it short and drove Jen to her apartment.

I said: "Be careful about who you open your door for, Jen."

"Why?" she asked. We knew each other well enough so that she could read me. We were still private people, but we were at the edge of more than that. I was sure that she knew there were things I wasn't telling her.

"Just be careful," I said lightly. "I wouldn't want someone to get in and steal you from me."

She looked away from me and opened the car door and I could see I'd offended her by the lightness. I caught her hand and she came back to me.

"I don't want to frighten you, Jen. All of this is serious business and I just want you to be careful." I kissed her and it made the world all right again for us—at least until she had time to go through it again.

"Yes," she said. She kissed me again. "I'll see you in the morning."

———◄◆►———

Robert Eugene Jolly operates his place on the river under the corporate name of "The Jolly Boatman." He sells all that one can use from luxury pleasure cruisers down to groceries to stock them. He has about half a mile of floating docks which he rents out for several dollars a foot per month to those in need of docking space.

He is known to his acquaintances as "Jolly." This name has nothing to do with his attitude, but is merely his last name. He is a serious man, a man of many committees, of hard work, of no play. Over the years he has run a peanut-sized operation up to a multi-million-dollar corporation. Now he is mid-fiftyish with suspiciously black hair, getting a little bit of a pot, but still a quick mover, very efficient.

We are friends. I was his lawyer before I went on the bench.

I walked down the riverbank and out on his dock. An old, very gray man watched my coming with suspicious eyes. A few boats were already in the river. In a couple of months there would be multitudes of them seeking their private party worlds away from it all. On this night the sounds of one loud party came from a big Chris-Craft down the dock.

"You looking for the party?" he asked.

"No. Where's Jolly?"

He looked me over and decided for me. "I guess maybe to Kiwanis or Chamber of Commerce or someplace. He usually comes back by this time of night to check things."

"Sounds like a good party," I said, glancing at the Chris-Craft.

"Been rollin' since yesterday," he said admiringly. "Some leaves, but others come." He looked up the bank. "Here comes Mr. Jolly."

Jolly came quickly down the bank. He grunted once at his employee and gave me a limp hand.

"How do, Jedge," he said. His voice was low. He kept it that way so that those who'd paid him no mind when he was poor could now strain to hear.

"Speak to you for a minute?" I asked.

He nodded. He looked at the Chris-Craft and raised an eyebrow to the old, gray man.

"No one's complained," the old man said. "But they're getting louder."

"Sheriff still aboard?" Jolly asked. I came to quick attention.

"I think maybe he left."

Jolly smiled and led me into his tiny office. It was very neat.

"What's up?"

"Is that the sheriff's boat?"

"I don't know. He came down and got on it, but so did

a lot of others. I went up and had my one drink with them. Then I butted out. They got some girls on there that wasn't convent-raised."

I wanted to ask him more questions about it, but he usually ran out of answers quickly.

"Was my bailiff, the one who got run over, down around here just before he got killed?"

He nodded. "He was out here on the dock one night not too long ago. Seems like I heard he got killed maybe the day after. I knew Ed pretty well. Too bad about him."

"Yes," I said. "What was he doing out here?"

"Said he was looking for a runaway who might be hid out on a boat. I told him to go ahead and look. I didn't see him for a while. He come back past the office and acted like he was happy as a bee in the puddin' and said he hadn't found his kid." He shook his head. "He was kind of dirty, like he'd been rummaging in a dusty closet. Wet night, too."

"Did he say anything else?"

"Said he was going up to the sheriff's office to report someone polluting the water and went grinning off into the night." He shook his head once more. "I thought maybe he was getting senile. Old enough, you know."

"What boats were here that night?"

"I don't know. Them that's here now. One or two transient boats."

"Do you keep a log?"

"Sure."

"Keep it someplace safe. And don't tell anyone I talked to you."

"Okay," he said. He snapped his fingers. "There's one

more thing. He said to tell anyone that asked that he'd been down on the dock."

"Did anyone ask?"

"Someone called is all. I don't know who it was."

"How soon after he left?"

"Not very long. Half an hour. About this time of night or a little later."

"Thanks, Jolly."

"For nothing. You got my vote even if having you on the bench does cost me an honest lawyer."

———◆———

I left half an hour early for the courthouse after a restless night. A spring storm had come up during the early hours and, never the soundest of sleepers, I'd spent a very long time listening to it, trying to separate its sounds into natural and those I suspected were not. Twice I'd padded about the house on stockinged feet, looking here, looking there, but finding nothing.

Half-a-man wasn't there when I arrived at the courthouse. To be unobtrusive about it I moved on inside and waited out of the way by the courthouse door. I nodded at jurors and courthouse employees as they arrived.

After about fifteen minutes of that, just as I was about to give it up, I saw Half come out of the cross street alley. He moved to the near edge of it, wary of traffic, then darted his cart like a streak across the traveled portion of the street. Samdog Cabel, whom I'd not seen waiting, came out of the shadows of the building and lifted Half up to the wall, then fled away into the shadows again.

I went outside.

"Mornin', Judge," he said. I could tell he was happier with me than he'd been in our last conversation. "You're out early." He pocketed my daily admission fee and then continued: "Thanks for helpin' me out of jail. Samdog said you come through for me." His eyes scanned the street and then came back to me. "I ain't going to forget it."

"How'd you come to find the billfold, Half?" I asked.

He looked around to make certain no one was listening. "I seen a guy throw it back there—or I *heard* him do it. I never actually seen him then, but I heard the billfold hit back there in the ashes. After things got quiet again I scooted back there and found it. There was still a fire going over in one corner of the incinerator, but the billfold was over away from it." He shook his head. "I found it fair. It should be mine. Now they took it. If I hadn't got it then it would have maybe burned up." He looked up at me. "Next day I mean."

"Didn't you know whose billfold it was?"

He shook his head strongly. "I ain't a fate tempter. I never read the papers, never listen to the radio. You hear bad things there. Sometimes I'll watch me a fight or a game on the TV, but I never listen to the bad time news no more. I just ignored everything in that billfold but the money."

In a way it made queer sense. He didn't exist at normal wave length. He operated in his own world, where the rules were different.

"How come you were here at night?" I asked.

"Sometimes I just stay around when the weather's good. It wasn't bad that night, kind of warm even."

"Did you see Ed that night?"

"Sure. I was up on the wall here. I wasn't paying any attention to him and him none to me. He come walking up from the river side and went past. He wasn't looking for me. Moving kind of purposeful. He went past without seeing me. Later, not much, but maybe five or ten minutes or so, I heard some sounds. I guess maybe it was eight or nine o'clock. I don't count time much. But it was full dark. When I heard the noises I turned to see what it was, but I didn't see nothin'."

"What noises did you hear?"

He shivered a little. "Like someone dropping a melon or something. Kind of a wet sound. Then it was quiet for a time, but I went on listening. I heard the billfold hit the incinerator. A time later, but not much, a car started up the alley behind where the incinerator is. It went out toward the other street. That was after a lot of doors slamming and like that."

"Is what you're telling me been told to them?"

"Who?"

"The officers who arrested you."

He gave me a funny look. "I didn't tell them anything. You remember what you told me before you was judge?"

"No." And I didn't. I'd told him a lot of things.

"I asked and you told me all I ever had to give them was my name and my address. That's just what I did. Then, when the judge down there in that clown court asked me what I was going to do, I said 'not guilty.'" He looked up at me. "Was that all right?"

"Sure it was." I nodded at him abstractedly, thinking about what he'd said. "Thanks for the information, Half."

He shrugged. "The whole thing was crazy. But it was a good thing that Samdog was home that night." The gloved hand lifted and the subject was changed. "Samdog tells me you're coming on. You've got a chance. I heard tell you went to a meeting they had Monday night and messed things up. Then I heard that some people leaving that meeting saw some of Sheriff Hen Zisk's bad ones throw some rocks at your car. Them that seen it have been spreading that around." He grinned up at me. "Been a lot of scurryin' and hurryin' going on in the opposition camp. Perry Bobbin hangs out at the sheriff's office a lot these days. I think you got them worried. Sheriff ought to worry, too. He's got troubles."

"That's good," I said, still thinking.

"Don't get your butt overconfident," he warned severely.

"Was there anyone else around on the wall or near it the night you found the billfold?" I asked.

He looked all around again. Then he leaned forward. "Samdog really was. He brought me up. But his people lied and said he was with them. I don't know where Samdog was." He pointed across the street at the string of three consecutive taverns. Already, in the early morning, there was traffic in front of them. One wag had pointed out that there was a tavern for plaintiffs, one for defendants, and a third for all the lawyers collectively. "Maybe he was across the street. He's been getting his wine at Eddo's." He shook his head confidently. "He wasn't involved, Samdog wasn't. I asked him."

Eddo's was the center tavern. I looked over and

thought I saw Samdog's shadowy form inside. "Ask him again if he saw or heard anything that night."

"Okay. But you know Samdog. He don't remember things very well. Especially dates and times."

———◆———

Upstairs I put on my robe, entered the courtroom, and got things going.

It was photo day. Prosecuting Attorney Allen Dunwich had put the police photographer on the stand first. He was a tall, spare man in his forties, wearing good clothes. He had a meticulous manner. Allen was having Jen mark the photos with identification numbers and then handing them on to his expert.

". . . And is this photograph I've just now given you, marked State's Exhibit 17, a fair and accurate representation of the scene inside the death room that you saw and photographed that fatal night?" he asked.

"Yes, sir, Mr. Dunwich."

Allen added it to the growing pile. The jury watched the pile and Allen curiously. George Higer sat sourly through the proceedings. I thought I knew what was in Higer's mind. The jury wanted to see the pictures. Dunwich was building suspense by having all of the pictures identified before offering them as evidence and asking that they be exhibited to the jurors. Higer could then object to at least a part of them on the grounds that they were repetitive and/or inflammatory, but when he did, then the jurors would believe that those which were withheld were far worse than those they saw. Human nature.

It was a losing proposition for Higer and he wasn't bearing it very stoically.

Later, to end open bickering, I called a recess and we picked out fourteen of the pictures for exhibit, making sure there was no repetition. It brought me a smile and a civil look from Higer. We reconvened and started the photos down the rows of eager juror fingers. Photos of the body at the hospital where the autopsy had been conducted, photos in the kitchen, close photos of the place of death. Janet Walker was the star of the photos and it was her last starring role. There she was for the jury to examine and to ponder that she would never grow older, that she was frozen in these last photographs into a final day in time.

On cross examination Higer got some minor revenge. He kept handing the photographer the individual pictures and asking him if those pictures showed whether or not the defendant, Amos Walker, was present in the pictures or had inflicted any of the injuries.

"Objection . . ." Allen Dunwich began.

I raised my eyebrows at him. "He's your witness, Mr. Dunwich, and this is cross examination."

Dunwich smiled amiably. "I'll withdraw the objection, but may I point out that no questions were asked this witness about the defendant and his whereabouts on the night of the killing and therefore I submit that cross examination concerning the defendant is improper."

I looked over at Higer. "I think perhaps he's about done with this witness, Mr. Dunwich."

Higer nodded and smiled.

But, of course, he wasn't really done. He kept moving

about, skirting the edges of the case, seeking chinks in the armor of the prosecution case from a witness who knew nothing more than he'd seen on the night he took photos. And the holes, gaping holes, became apparent. The cold killer does his work purposefully without an audience. Even the killer who does his murder in heat seldom invites a large crowd. And so there were gaps.

We wrangled the day through and I broke it mercifully at just after four o'clock. Jen and I went into the office and waited out the crowd, then closed things when the last of them got away. Outside I saw television cameras from across the river. We would be on the news tonight.

Downstairs the halls were deserted, but a light still emanated from the recorder's door. I braked us there.

Gosport grinned at me.

"Hi there, lady," he said admiringly to Jen. He nodded at me. "How goes your big trial, Judge Mickey?"

"As well as it can, I hope."

"Think it'll finish by next Tuesday?"

"It might. No way to say."

"Couldn't you push it along?"

"No. I won't do that. Why? What do you hear?"

"You're coming on some," he said. "If Amos got convicted you'd be a cinch. If the trial is still going on, then I don't know. Close." He raised a hand to forestall questions. "I think you'll probably get beat, but some things sound good. More people than you can believe either saw what happened when we drove away from the meeting or are claiming they saw it. The word got around town *fast.*" He looked away from me. "Trouble with Amos's people is that they's too abrupt, maybe like Amos. Amos is tough.

I'm older than him by maybe ten years, but I'm young enough to have been kicking it around in his time." He shook his head remembering those days. "He's always been a mean son of a bitch, Amos has. Maybe he would use a club or something. I've kept trying and sometimes, inside my head, I can see him beating her to death." He looked up at me again. "What is it he's supposed to have used?"

"Prosecution claims a blunt instrument, a club maybe, or something like a club," I said guardedly.

He shook his head. "His wife was running with Hen Zisk, I've heard."

"The sheriff?" I asked. Discomfort was growing inside me. I was hearing evidence of a sort outside where I should be hearing it. I'd have to ignore it as far as the trial was concerned.

"Couple of people have told me that. Claim they saw Hen's car parked up there a few nights before his missis was killed."

"I see."

"Nobody saw Hen, 'cause he's slick, but he parked his car maybe a block down a side street." He brayed laughter. "Old Amos off to a meeting and Hen taking care of his homework for him. Amos wouldn't be so strong for Hen if he knew about that."

Jen touched my arm as she realized the situation I was in was becoming more and more uncomfortable.

"We've got to go, Gosport," she said.

9

Threats

That night the anonymous caller finally spoke to me on the phone: "You keep your nose straight ahead, Judge, or you'll lose it. You keep on messing around and running around and doing what ain't your business and maybe that pretty baby sister of yours won't be so pretty or maybe you'll come home and find your mother unhorsed from out of her chair."

I could feel the cold coming up from my feet, threatening to envelop me completely.

"What exactly am I not supposed to do?" I asked.

"You just keep on with what you're supposed to be doing, trying Mr. Amos. No one really cares about that. That's all right. But you stop right there. You let it rest. Run your damned court. Divorce people. Make speeches. But quit sticking your nose into trouble or you'll find it the way that your simple bailiff did."

Somehow the voice sounded vaguely familiar. Maybe I was hearing it through a handkerchief.

"Someone turned on a gas jet in the basement," I said. "Was that you?"

"Guilty as charged," he said, and laughed. He rehung the phone.

I went to bed angry and lay there in knots, twisting and turning. I couldn't be around the house all of the time and I couldn't have guards at the house during the time when I wasn't there. A patient watcher would find his opportunity. I wondered about someplace where I could send Mom and Annie while this was going on. There were some relatives in Indianapolis, but Mom despised them. I explored several ideas, but each of them broke down under close examination. Mom would die away from her house. She would wilt and sicken. I'd seen it before.

I wondered briefly about how the caller knew what I'd been doing, but I'd made no real secret of it. I hadn't made an open examination of anything, but I'd asked a lot of questions, been some places, evinced interest. Someone had noticed.

They'd noticed Ed, too. Then his head had been beaten in and he'd been discarded like a bug removed from a windshield. One wipe and he was gone.

I had no doubt that my caller and his people (if any) were in earnest. The whole thing made me feel a mixture of two things. I was afraid. I was angry. I shook the two feelings together into one massive frustration.

Once, a few years back now, I'd been able to sleep at nights and still come immediately awake and ready if

there was a change in the world around me, and so I'd
survived. Maybe it was a gift I'd not entirely lost. I hoped
so. I slept, but came awake twice, once when a soft and
gentle rain began to fall and the second time when the
milkman entered the yard.

I was encouraged. Both of those times I came awake
completely, arm stub tingling.

———◆———

Coulson, the house bailiff, came early enough for me to
get away ahead of time. We grinned at each other.

"I ain't seen anything which looks suspicious, Judge,"
he said. He hefted a heavy caliber, short-barreled rifle.
"Me'n your mom talk some. I used to know your father
when I was growing up. He used to give me apples."

We shook hands and I went on out the door. Mom was
at the window watching. I got out the Monte Carlo and
decided to drive to the Hickory Hills section to the area
where Ed's body was found. From the news accounts and
what I'd heard I had an idea of the location and I slowed
in that block. In a side lot high school boys played a lack-
adaisical game of catch with a baseball. Others watched
from the corner, boys and girls. A burning cigarette or
roach passed from hand to hand and eyes watched me
suspiciously when I slowed and parked the car.

I got out and walked toward the group on the corner
and was ignored by them.

When I was upon them I asked, in a loud voice: "Did
anyone here know Ed Long?"

No one looked at me.

"I heard they found his body right around here in the street somewhere," I said.

A boy looked at me and I recognized his face vaguely. It was young and unformed and I'd seen it in juvenile court. Someone Ed had brought in and introduced gravely, not one who'd been in bad trouble. He gave me a look and threw the ball to someone else. There was contempt in the look, but it seemed to me that there was also fear.

"Deal me out," he said to the other ball throwers. His voice was deeper than I would have expected. He said to me: "Better go away."

"Someone else will be back with me if I leave now," I said reasonably.

"Tell him to go suck, Sambo," a boy's voice said from far away. It was a halfhearted voice, not in dead earnest. Maybe, at night, it would not have been. Alienation grows.

Sambo shook his head. "We don't know nothing." He looked up at me. "I swear it, Judge," he said, admitting recognition, making me a person. "Ed was okay out here. He gave me my driver's license back that day he brought me to your office. And he didn't have to do it." He nodded at the street. "When they found him here we all talked about it. No one heard anything. No one seen anything. I mean it."

"All right," I said.

"We all agreed if anyone admitted to seeing anything or hearing anything that we'd call the police anonymous and lay it on them. But there ain't nothin'."

I nodded and waited, sure there was more.

He said: "You can hear cars pretty good at night." He smiled without humor. "The walls where I live ain't very thick. And I know lots of guys who wind it up hard. There's a straight run up the street for maybe five, six blocks. A lot of guys heard things like that—motors revving, tires squealing, brakes, around the time Mr. Long was supposed to have been mashed, but no screams, no nothing like that."

"Thank you," I said.

He gave me a surprised look, almost embarrassed. He turned away and someone threw him the ball. He passed it back.

I went across the street to the car. When I was about half a block away I saw a yellow school bus stopped at the corner and the kids entering it for another day in the jungle.

I wasn't at my best that day during the trial. I was sleepy and irritable, but it was a common day in the case at trial. More chain of custody type day. Allen Dunwich spent most of it going down the custody line in his various items already introduced, showing to the jury that nothing had changed, what hands the items had passed through between the time they'd been discovered, marked and held for evidence, and the date of today. The jury listened in fascination, never having seen this sort of thing before. I sat in my swivel chair and fretted the morning away. Now and then I could see Amos Walker casting side glances at me and I wondered if I was being inspected for signs of pressure. I was sure he knew that I was being pushed at, but I wondered if he knew the attitude of those who were pressuring. They had not seemed to care about his predicament.

I kept remembering Coulson, the bailiff, guarding the house. Once, while I was into that, Jen looked up at me and gave me a tiny wink from her court stenographer's table below me and, as the day wore on, by rationalizing, I found it hard to stay with a sense of dread. I was living in America the beautiful, with police all around me, more police every year. I was doing useful work. Surely I had nothing to fear.

Outside the windows of the courtroom I saw the day turn dark and rain began to fall, but then the sun came back out in the late afternoon.

I admonished the jury about discussing the case among themselves before hearing all the evidence, the arguments of counsel and my instructions. I sent them off for their supper and for their motel rooms. They filed past me smiling, seemingly enjoying their vacationlike time.

"I need a drink," I whispered to Jen.

She gave me her very best smile. "I herewith accept your offer, if you mean you're buying."

We impatiently waited out the lawyers, did our paper work, and then adjourned to Peter's Pub. I don't often go there and I had a feeling that Gosport wouldn't approve just now, but we went anyway. I couldn't go inside without a slight feeling of guilt. It's all right for judges to drink in private clubs and at parties, but the world doesn't smile at a judge who drinks often in public places. But the Elks would have Allen Dunwich in for his nightly infusion and I didn't want to have to endure him any more right now. We had, over the days, worn each other out for a while. Maybe I was leaning over too far to keep things fair.

He'd recover.

We sat ourselves down in the back of Peter's Pub under the big, old, slowly turning fans that the management refused to remove. We drank very dry martinis made with bar gin and very little vermouth.

"What's wrong?" Jen asked. "You've seemed very snappish today."

I debated what to tell her and then did tell her some things. I told her about the telephone calls. She was close to me and I owed her that. It was very possible that threats made about Mom and Annie could extend to her.

"You've had calls like that before," she said sensibly, when I was done.

I nodded. "True."

"Then why get upset over these?"

"They seem to know everything that I'm doing—or at least someone does. And I've got a problem in trying to protect those I need to keep safe. I've got me a part-time bailiff at my house now. I wonder how much money it would take to get to him? I used to get calls offering me money. I can't believe that money might not do the trick that needs doing for them."

"Not with Coulson, I think," she said.

I shrugged. "I hope you're right. I suppose he's as good as any."

"Offer him the job as bailiff when this is over. I mean permanently."

"If I win?"

She nodded.

"Whoever it is doesn't seem to care much about Amos—at least not yet," I mused. "And I guess Coulson is as all right as I can find. In this town I could never be sure that anyone I hired wouldn't take off at the first sign of trouble or, worse, get signed up by the opposition."

She gave me a level look. "Well, don't worry your head about me. I think I can probably take care of myself."

"How about against Chili Blackwell, if he should come calling? Or someone who came to your door you didn't know? Someone plausible?"

She thought for a minute. "I'll just keep my door locked and chained. And I'll be extra careful."

"Sure you will," I said dismally, knowing that her answer wasn't a valid one. There were too many doors, too many windows.

I was nervous, it was after five, so I took her on home and, after a short, sweet time, I let her lock and chain the door behind me.

I went home and relieved Coulson, who was waiting in a sheltered place in the hall. I noticed that his eyes still were wide open and his movements with the gun were quick and sure.

I said: "If I get re-elected how'd you like to wind up being permanent bailiff?"

He gave me a slow smile and a nod.

The phone rang at ten and I picked it up warily. I thought maybe it would be Mr. Anonymous again, but it was not. It was Captain Tiny Quinn.

"I've some news for you. The state boys found Chili Blackwell in a barn two counties north this afternoon. He had your name and address in his pocket and he had a gun. But no one will have to worry about him any more. He was dead. The deputy I talked to up there said the doc who examined the body said he was eaten up with cancer. Remember how big he was?"

I remembered. Two hundred plus pounds. I said so.

"They weighed him at the morgue. He weighed less than a hundred and twenty pounds. Anyhow, he's dead." He paused for a long moment, while I thought. "I figured maybe you'd want to know. Make for better sleeping."

"Not really," I said. "It seems I've got some other problems if what you're saying is that Chili never made it here."

"My bet is he didn't. Why would he then go to another county? What's your other problems?" He cackled. "Other than the election."

"I've been looking around a little on Ed Long. Someone doesn't like it. I had a call last night threatening me and my family. Then there have been some other things."

"What kind of things?"

I told him about the intruder in the basement and the earlier, silent calls.

"I'm interested in what you've found out about Ed Long," he said. "Something there must have set off the threats."

"Maybe," I said. "I really don't know a lot. I know Ed was into the drug trade around here, but that was nothing new. And I think maybe he got aboard a boat down at Jolly's dock and maybe dumped something into the river there, most probably on the night he was killed. Heroin or cocaine. Expensive stuff."

"I'll take a look at the boat. What name?"

"I guess I'm not much at this. I didn't look. A big Chris-Craft docked at Jolly's. Only one like it there. And use some care, Captain. It might belong to the high sheriff, Hen Zisk."

"I'll set a watch on it. Did you find anything in Ed's papers at your office?"

"No—nothing that didn't lead right back to where I am right now," I said, suddenly realizing there was a place I'd not yet looked. An obvious place.

"I'd like to give you some guards," he said, "but it isn't my decision. I've heard around here that a lot of our people have been told not to work for you even on their own time." He sighed. "I drive past your place now and then. And I know Coulson. He's a good one."

"Thank you, Captain. And thanks for calling me about Chili."

After a while I went upstairs and turned on my light. Whoever it was must have been waiting for that. It was maybe eleven at night, dark outside, the wind still for once.

I heard a car brake hard out in the street and I heard the motor turning softly without any sound of movement.

I had a bad premonition. I went to the closet and got the loaded shotgun and a few extra shells. I looked at those shells closely for the first time. Bird shot. They might stop a man close up, but all they'd do at any distance was anger him.

The first shot came through my window, shattering glass, shredding the blind. It was followed by several more.

I left the room and ran toward the curving stairs. Behind me a shot blew my ceiling light to bits while I was coming down the steps.

I got to my front door and slid it open after fumbling a bit with the lock. I rolled out the door, staying in the shadows of the pillars, twisting and turning to the edge of the porch. My clothes felt too tight on me and I was sweating.

My assailant was far out in the yard, past the hedge, too far for a good shot. He was a dark shadow against other shadows. He fired more shots into my darkened window. I shot in the general direction of the hedge and got a return shot that splintered the pillar far above my head.

The car was visible in the street, sitting there near our curb, motor ticking over, waiting for him to flee.

I shot at it once and heard the windshield go. I reloaded and gave it two more, spattering it good. The motor began to miss a little.

I reloaded once more with the last two shells I had with me. There were more upstairs, but they'd do me little good now. Inside the house I could hear movement. Mom and Annie.

"Stay down in there," I called loudly. "I'm out here on the porch."

Down the street, lights were coming on in several houses.

Out front the car sputtered and died. The rifleman tried again to pick me out on the porch, but I stayed behind my pillar and his shooting was very bad. I let one last load go at him, saving the other. His firing stopped and, in a bit, I heard the sound of running feet. He was moving away from the direction of the lighted houses, abandoning his car.

I waited some more. Inside I could hear Mom calling to Annie, then calling my name.

"I'm okay, Mom. I'm out on the porch. Stay away from the windows and don't turn on any lights." I could envision her rolling out onto the front porch in her wheel chair.

But whoever it was had vanished down the street. There were no more shots.

I went back into the house. I endured the police who came to investigate. I learned that the car was a stolen one from across the river. I told the story three times. Finally, I slept on the couch.

In the morning I ate a careful breakfast. Mom had a million questions and I had no real answers for her. Out front a uniformed trooper sat in a marked state police car. Another similar vehicle toured the area, passing in front slowly now and then.

When Coulson came I told the story one more time. He listened and nodded at correct places.

"You mind if I sleep here for a few nights, Judge?" he asked when I was done.

"Can you?"

"Yes. I got a little farm, but my wife's dead going on three years. My boy does most of the farming these days and he can make do without me for a while. So, if it ain't out of line, I'll stay."

"I'd appreciate it."

———◆———

The weather had turned warm. I drove to Ed's house, where he'd lived with his half sister. It was in the Groves area of town. Once there'd been orchards there before the housing contractors gobbled it up.

I knew Ed's half sister a little and remembered seeing her at the funeral home and funeral.

I parked the car in front of the house. The subdivision was old enough so that shade trees had grown replacing the old fruit trees and I walked past them and up a carefully tended yard path.

The house was boxy and two stories high. There was a one-story porch all along the front and, despite the fact that the hour was still early, an old lady sat swinging in a chained swing. Her hands were primly clamped together and she moved carefully and easily, a shawl around her shoulders. I knew she was almost twenty years older than Ed and that her husband had gone off to an old war and never returned. I remembered also that Ed had said that her memory was bad and that she was "failing." I wondered how she was living now.

"Hello, Mrs. Shumate," I said from the walk.

Her birdlike eyes surveyed me and recognized me.

"Come up and set, Judge," she said hoarsely. She nodded toward a rocker near the swing.

I sat down and waited.

"I miss Eddie," she said softly. "Sometimes, in the late afternoons, I forget he's not here any more and I make tea for both of us and then I find the extra cup in the mornings when I'm better."

"I miss him also," I said.

She gave me a look full of curiosity. "He liked you, Judge." She shook her head gently, as if trying to reason about why he'd liked me.

"I miss Eddie," she said again.

I had a moment's empathy with her. She'd had this little life, safe and secure. By all her planning, she should have long preceded him in death. Then, suddenly, it had not been that way and she was trying to cope with the change in situation without any real ability to do it. I decided I'd contact someone and have them watch her and make certain she was all right—or as all right as she would ever be now that the last dream had died.

"I'm trying to find out some reason why someone might have been after him—wanted to hurt him," I said. "Did he ever talk to you about anyone like that?"

She shook her head. "No. Ed didn't have many enemies. He was sheriff for two terms and managed to get through that and I thought it was over. Then he went to work for you."

"Yes. He worked with the kids."

"Eddie liked kids. And even after all the stories in the newspapers kids still call here wanting to talk with him."

"Did you find anything in his room after he was—gone?" I asked. "Any papers. Anything at all?"

She pursed her lips. "Funny you should ask, Judge. Very strange. Someone came into the house while I was at the funeral home. Must have been watching for me to leave. Went rooting through his room throwing things here and there, taking his papers. I never said anything to any of those nice police officers. Ed's name was enough in the news without there being any more." She nodded. "There was an envelope with your name on it. It was on his dresser. I saw it there and meant to bring it to the funeral home, but I guess I just plain forgot it." She shook her head dolefully. "Sometimes I do forget. I'm sorry."

I smiled at her. "That's all right, Mrs. Shumate. Whoever broke in got the envelope?"

She nodded, still not happy about having forgotten it. I wanted to see his room. "Mrs. Shumate . . ." I began.

"Call me Maude," she said. "Ed always called me Maude. We were the last two left in the family." She looked away from me.

"Could I look in his room, Maude?" I asked. "Maybe they missed something."

"I don't think they did, but you can look," she said. "You go on in. It's the first door at the top of the steps. I'll just wait out here." She smiled without real meaning. "Seems a lot like spring today."

"Yes," I said. It was warmer.

"I ration my trips up those stairs," she explained. She went back to swinging gently, and, with that as final permission, I entered the house and went up the unrailed stairs.

Ed's room was out of his past—like mine. The bed was an old four-poster, piled with several mattresses so that even a tall man would have to hop up to it. Window shades, browning at the edges, were drawn over the two windows, but it was light enough to see. There was a battered bureau and a nightstand. A second door opened to a closet full of Ed's clothes. One whole wall of the room plus part of another wall were covered with framed photos.

I looked in the bureau and nightstand, even taking the drawers out and looking behind and under them. I felt a little foolish doing it, but I did it anyway.

Nothing.

I inspected the clothes in the closet and checked every pocket. Nothing again.

I examined the photos, letting up one of the shades a bit so that it was easier to see. Most of the pictures featured Ed in one of his several careers: fire marshal for the state, city councilman, police officer, deputy sheriff, sheriff, bailiff-probation officer. I stood with him in one of the bailiff-probation officer photos. I'd forgotten it being taken, but now, seeing the picture, I remembered. We'd stood out by the trees on the courthouse lawn and an obliging Jen had snapped Ed and me shaking hands there. She'd used Ed's old camera. I wondered what had happened to it. And I also remembered the album of pictures I'd brought home from the office. I'd forgotten to show them to Mom.

I went carefully down the rows of pictures. At the end of one row there was a vacant spot, a place where a hook was still in the wall, but which had no picture hanging thereon.

I looked back at the preceding picture. What I'd seen so far indicated that the pictures were hung in some sort of time sequence and the picture preceding the missing one showed Ed standing in front of the sheriff's residence talking to another uniformed officer. I leaned closer. The other officer was Hen Zisk, who'd been his chief deputy and then run against Ed and beaten him.

I wondered what had happened to the missing picture.

I double checked the room and then went back downstairs. Maude still rocked idly in her swing, dreaming of other days. She smiled vaguely when she saw me come out the door.

"What happened to Ed's camera?" I asked.

"I gave it away. There was a boy up the street who liked Ed. I gave it to him."

"Then there's a picture missing from the wall. Did you notice that?"

She shook her head. "No. I don't see things real good. I never paid much attention to his pictures except to dust around them." She saw that I was ready to go on and was alarmed. "Must you go so quickly? Set and talk just a little more."

I looked at my watch. Still a few minutes to court time. I sat down again and let her tell me what it had been like with Ed around, but I already knew that anyway.

10

Closing Remarks

The defendant rested his case the following Friday noon after a parade of character witnesses of doubtful value. In the early afternoon the state presented some very minor rebuttal evidence, wherein police officers, whose testimony concerning Amos's demeanor when he was arrested had been contradicted by the defendant, testified again.

After that was done, suddenly there was time.

Time to ask the jurors if they'd prefer coming in Saturday or waiting until Monday to receive the case. Surprisingly, they voted to resume Monday. That got partially more easy to understand when the bailiff took the jury out to their secluded motel. From my office, where Higer and Al Dunwich were querulously arguing instructions, I could see the two unmarried jurors, one the female schoolteacher, the other the convalescing male engineer, go down the hall holding hands.

Allen saw it too. He nudged Higer.

"That's a block vote," he said.

Higer did a double take and shook his head.

I sat in my office the rest of Friday afternoon as they argued instructions. Outside, in Jen's office, she waited patiently, typing changes that were agreed on or ordered.

We got done a little before four o'clock. Higer went off with Dunwich for a drink. They were mellowing toward each other. It happens that way during a trial when two lawyers are fairly equal in ability.

I closed the office door thankfully behind them and kissed Jen and the damned phone picked that moment to ring.

I answered. It was Judge File.

"Stop past and see me," he ordered.

"In a bit," I agreed. I rehung the phone and looked at Jen. It was better to think about her than it was Judge File.

"I've got to stop down and see File. Can you go on by yourself and meet me at the Elks?"

She nodded, not aggrieved. She redid her lipstick and moved out. I locked up and followed her down the hall. Judge File awaited me in his office.

"I hear you had some trouble," he began. "Something about a juvenile shooting through your window."

"I heard that's what Perry Bobbin is trying to spread," I said. "But the gentleman with the gun looked full grown to me."

He shook his head. "I've never had a problem like that in all my years on the bench." He said it stoutly, as if I'd somehow committed a wrong.

"Bully for you," I said. I waited.

"How's your trial going?" he asked finally.

"All right. It will go to the jury Monday."

"What's your guess?"

I shrugged. He knew as much about it as I did. I decided on candor.

"It's a tossup. Thin, all circumstantial. But a jury can believe Amos guilty and very well may believe it." I looked at him without expression. "Amos testified in his own behalf."

"I heard him," he said, looking away. "And I heard some of the cross. Allen Dunwich did a hatchet job on him."

I remembered:

Dunwich: Mr. Walker, can't you admit to this jury that you several times considered killing your wife?

Walker: No, I can't admit that because it ain't true.

Dunwich: Wasn't she a drunk? Sometimes unfaithful? Didn't you fight? Argue?

Walker: Yes. I was going to get around to divorcing her sometime, I guess.

Dunwich: Did you talk to a lawyer about a divorce?

Walker (smiling grimly): Lots of lawyers. All the good ones. The only one in town I guess I didn't bother to see was maybe you.

Dunwich (smiling and unruffled): Did you discuss with these many lawyers what it might cost you in money and prestige to get yourself your divorce?

Walker: We talked some about it.

Dunwich: And weren't you warned that she might try to take you—hold you up?

Higer (standing up): Privileged, Your Honor.

Dunwich: Withdrawn. Now, Mr. Walker, on direct examination you admitted to being a violent man, didn't you?

Walker: I've had me a few fights in my time, laddie.

Dunwich: Estimate how many for the jury.

Walker: None I lost.

Dunwich: And you figured yourself a good way not to lose this one. You thought you could get away with it, didn't you?

Walker: No, I didn't do it. (He peered around the courtroom, his face a mixture of arrogance and uneasiness, sensing the feeling of the jury toward him.) Someone else came in and got her. Someone else did it.

Dunwich: Then tell the jury about the coat, Mr. Walker. Tell them why it was down in the basement, back of the furnace.

Walker: I didn't put it there.

It had gone on like that for a very long time, Amos getting madder and madder, Dunwich baiting him ever harder. The jury could see that Amos would very much like to have Dunwich dead. They'd have the weekend to mull that over.

I came back to now.

Judge File was looking at me. I could read very little in his eyes. I thought he'd asked a question and I'd missed it.

"What was it?" I asked.

He said: "It still isn't too late for you, Mickey. I know lots of people in the party who'd switch over to you in a second if Amos gave them one little word. If Amos was out of here on Tuesday morning running the election I can virtually assure you there'd be no trouble at all." He raised a hand to cut off my answer. "Think about it. Higer will refile his motion for a directed verdict on Monday morning. It's routine at this point. If you granted that motion everything would be smooth again."

"You think maybe the janitorial people might even clean up my end of the hall?" I asked innocuously.

He gave me a quick glance, not sure whether I was in jest or not.

I smiled at him. "I think maybe sometime when I come in here I ought to wire myself for sound."

He colored. "Don't be more of an idiot than you already are."

"I may be an idiot, but I'm not for sale or trade for money or votes. It would seem that ought to be getting damned apparent by now."

He shrugged. "I just want you to be reasonable. If you aren't, then maybe, six months or a year from now, when it's all quiet again, someone drops a bomb in your living room or shoots your kid sister."

"Are you threatening me, Judge?"

"Not at all. And I'm not asking you to do anything crooked. What we're talking about is a case that can go either way. Grant the motion and you could be a hero. Amos owns the news here." He looked at me. "Do you really think Amos is guilty?"

"That isn't for me to decide. That's what his jury is for. The state's presented a prima-facie case."

"Promise me you'll think about it," he said smoothly. "Believe that no one asked me to see you." He spread his hands. "I'm not a bad man. I never took a dime in my life. But I've been in politics long enough to be practical."

I stood up and looked down at him, slouched behind his desk. I thought he wasn't being truthful when he said he wasn't on the take. There are lots of ways to be on it. The careful gift at Christmas, the invitation to take part in a venture for profit. He lived too high, took an overlot of vacations, spent much time at the area horse tracks, and bet many dollars there.

"All this is destroying the party," he said morosely. "That's what I'm concerned about."

"The party can stomach a lot," I said. "In this primary, for example, I've had reports that some of the precinct people are ready to vote the dead ones, a few thousand dollars is available to buy the drunk vote, and the good sheriff will put the arm on anyone who causes an unanticipated problem at any polling place—a problem he didn't plan," I said. "Tell him for me that if he gets over the line I personally will see he has his own problems." I turned away.

"You're a bastard," he said to my back.

"My own bastard," I said. "Not yours, not his." I turned back to him. "Don't call me that again. In fact, just don't call me at all."

I went on out of his office stiffly and down the steps. Outside the day was warm and there was still an hour of sun left in it. Instead of driving I walked to the Elks Club, and instead of walking through the business district, I went down a side street. I walked past aristocratic, old houses built to the edge of the sidewalk, Federal style.

They were houses out of another time. Seeing them and the walk helped work off my anger.

My town was old. Once, there'd been no bridges and we'd competed fiercely for river trade with the now bulging city across the river. Things were no longer that way. They'd won that old trade war and then bridges had joined us together. Their problems were ours. Sometimes I had good dreams about blowing up the spans we now had—while interstate officials discussed yet more co-operative bridges. With the bridges down the inevitable might be delayed—the time when it all crashed down over there and the strong hunted the weak to extinction and then craftily and bloodily stalked each other.

Soon.

———◆———

Jen sat with Allen and Ellen Dunwich at the Elks. Allen lifted a festive glass to me when I approached.

"What did you do with Higer?" I asked.

"He's a good lawyer, but he's candy. One drink and forward gear across the river," he said. His tensions were gone. All that he need now do was sum up for a jury and await the outcome. Trial over.

"I cut Amos a new one," he said softly to me, lifting his martini beaker and staring through it in fascination. "I shall be a folk hero among my tribe."

"Doubles are very bad for folk-hero types," his wife said. She was smiling.

Jen and I held hands under the table.

"Heard anything new on Ed?" I asked Allen.

He shook his head.

"Funny how he got killed right up there in the court-house yard, no more than fifty yards from the sheriff's office," I said darkly.

"Maybe your good friend, Sheriff Zisk, let Amos out of his cage and Amos bopped Ed over the head with the same weapon he used on his wife," Allen offered. "Or maybe the good sheriff did the job himself."

"Could of been anyone," I said.

He nodded. "Right. And I've been so hooked up in this I really haven't looked hard at that. Besides, I only prosecute them—not catch them."

"I think maybe the problem was that Ed deep-sixed a cache of drugs into the river. Then he told someone about it. After that he was killed, carted away, and dumped out in Hickory Hill. Maybe someone was watching him, following him."

"Well, I do know he wasn't in the sheriff's office the night he was killed. He never made it that far."

I waited.

"He was in there the night before he was killed. He wanted to talk to the sheriff. He wound up talking to Joe Pierceton and promised he'd come back. He never did. Then he got it the next night."

I thought about that. Something nibbled at the edge of my consciousness again, something gray and greasy.

"He wasn't in the sheriff's office the night he got killed —at least no one in there will admit he was—according to Tiny Quinn." He shook his head. "The only one you can usually get a straight answer from at the sheriff's is Joe Pierceton and he wasn't there."

"No found weapon on the death of Janet Walker. None on Ed Long," I mused.

"That's not unusual."

I thought about it some more, reaching for things which vanished as I got close.

He signaled a cruising waitress for more drinks. I protested, but weakly. Friday.

"They say we plot here," Allen said, grinning.

"Who says? Who plots?"

"You and me plot. They call us the 'purity pair.' Your good companion and opponent Perry L. Bobbin is the main teller of such tales." He shook his head. "He's, of course, attempting to make it appear as if we're in things together and out to get Amos." He shook his head again. "There were times during the trial I thought it was the other way."

"All in the cause of fairness and a clean appeal transcript, Allen."

He grinned. "I know. I know." He looked away and then back. "Look around carefully Tuesday when you go to the polls. You may see some strange things, Judge."

"Tell me what to look for." Although I was trying, for the moment, to forget the upcoming primary, it was difficult for me to do so.

"Amos's people have been busily hauling in some of the bums and voting them absentee in the clerk's office. The big push will come on Tuesday. The sheriff and Perry and Randy will have their helpers out in force hauling them in and paying them off. I'd say maybe four hundred votes and you'll not get 5 per cent of them."

Gosport had warned me that such was sure to happen and it was something I'd already found I could live with.

So it was illegal? No one cared much—except me this time.

"I'm going to try to get you close to even—maybe," Allen continued. "We've got no contests on my side of the fence—it's hard enough to even get folks to run much less get others to run against them. So some of our people will vote in your primary." He smiled. "Wait and see what happens." He stopped and thought for a moment. "Just don't get yourself killed between now and then."

"Guess for me on the outcome, Allen."

"I wouldn't know and am a poor guesser. I shouldn't have been elected, but was. Voters seem to be getting a bit smarter. Maybe there's hope for the system yet. A few weeks ago I'd have bet you were a loser. You still may be one, but it will be close."

I sipped my drink and thought some more, aware of Jen's hand in mine. I was a man without many outside interests. I liked to drink a little. I liked to watch TV Westerns and an occasional Reds baseball game. Except for Mom and Annie and now, Jen, I had nothing but the job. I'd lost myself in it and I dreaded losing it. I'd survived the early, veiled bribe offers (which seemingly, à la Judge File, hadn't stopped), the semi-threats, the distrust of those in the courthouse. I'd ignored raised eyebrows, the silent treatment from some, and offices that got dirtier and dirtier. I'd survived the attempt on my life, which had yet to be reported in the local paper or radio station.

I had a frustrated feeling knowing that nothing I could do now would make any significant difference. The organization was rolling. They were going to throw me out as an example, as a punishment. I could go out and shake hands and smile at people, but I was a bad smiler/shaker and such might lose me more than it would gain.

The thing to do was to wait it out and hope I won—and never show a thing if I lost. The taste of the martini turned bitter as I thought about that.

I cut off those martinis before too much damage had been done and left. I took Jen to her place and dropped her there after a long while. I waited in the hall until she'd locked and bolted her door.

I sat around the darkened living room with Mom and Annie and Coulson, all of us too silent, all of us striving, but never gaining gayness. We watched television.

Are you done out there?

———————◆————————

I dreamed.

In the dream Ed was alive. He smiled at me and led me by the hand. He took me up a wet path, but I saw no rain. He pointed out some sights along the wavery way. There was a car with a crumpled fender and a rusted bumper. There was a huge boat which loomed up out of darkness so that only the topmost deck could be seen. A lady on the boat looked down and laughed at me. I recognized her eyes. Amos's wife—Janet.

A man with a long gun waited in the shadow, but Ed only laughed, first at the man with the gun, then at me.

The world around me was sunless, cold, dank. And I knew the man with the gun even though he had no face.

I awoke. The cold and the damp were real. I'd covered the bullet-broken window with cardboard, but the night wind had partially stripped it away and blown my door shut. I got up and pushed the cardboard tight again, staying away from the opening itself for fear that someone watched and waited outside. When the cardboard was secure I opened the hall door and felt a welcome rush of warm air.

I crept through the house without turning on lights. There was nothing. Outside, as I watched away from the windows of the sunroom, I saw a state police car pass the house. They could not guard us forever. Judge File was right about that.

I went back upstairs to my own room. I'd stayed there mostly because of stubbornness. I wasn't going to be run from my own room.

My eyes had become accustomed to the half darkness. I could make out the holes in the walls and in the ceiling. Two bullet-smashed pictures had vanished during the day, probably claimed by Mom. One was me in a Scout uniform, the other was high school graduation with Randy Rumple next to me.

I examined the room for perhaps the hundredth time and saw again that the holes were all high in the walls or in the ceiling. The rifleman had fired in an upward trajectory, but from a substantial distance. His shots had, of course, angled up.

Only the top windowpane was broken.

I remembered again the call from Mr. Anonymous. He hadn't seemed much concerned with Amos Walker and his plight. That lack of concern might only be a ploy to remove suspicion from Amos. Maybe my caller really had no interest, or maybe his interest was adverse to Amos.

My bad marksman might be a very good marksman firing carefully. His abandoned car had yielded nothing.

I tossed about in bed, wrinkling the sheets, pulling my covers free. The wind came up again and blew the door closed and I let it stay that way and lay in the cold punishing myself because no light would come.

Saturday morning.

I remembered the album of photos and called Gosport McFay and asked him to stop by. He came in the early afternoon and I had him look over the album. I'd already had Mom look it over. She'd had no useful comment.

Gosport went through it earnestly, jaws moving as he gazed at the pictures. Annie came by the living room door once, saw him, and bolted for her room upstairs.

"A lot of old faces," Gosport said. "I remember most of the folks in there."

I pointed: "Is that Amos?"

He nodded. "Long time ago."

"Does anything in the album mean a nickel's worth to you?" I waited for a moment. "I mean as far as Ed getting killed?"

"Nope. Ed was always taking pictures or getting someone to take pictures with him in them—all his life." He smiled thinly. "Sometimes, if he got real mad at someone —really wrote them off—he'd tear up any pictures he had of them."

"I see."

"Not always, though. I seen him do it one time when he was young when a girl he went with threw him over."

"If there was a picture gone from Ed's wall it could then either mean he'd destroyed it or it had been taken?" I asked.

"Or mean nothing at all."

"Is there anyone not in the album who maybe ought to be there?"

"Not that I can think of." He looked down at the album. "I bet Ed took a hundred pictures for every one that's here. He just kind of put the best ones in here—representative photos from the various time zones he lived in and through. So about everyone Ed knew is in here."

"How about Randy Rumple?"

"No. I didn't see him, but he and Ed weren't ever close. Most of the pictures predate the time he might have met Randy. But Amos is in them, Hen Zisk, Perry L. Bobbin, Judge File—you and me—everyone important."

I thought about that for a moment, but nothing came into my head, no new ideas.

Gosport put the album down. He was beginning to look pained. I went to the kitchen and got him an old, empty tin can.

"I'll take it with me and get rid of it," he said apologetically. "I know your sis don't like my chewing, but I'm too old to change."

He moved on to a new subject: "I got someone to work for you at every precinct but your own. If you're still in trial and the day is fair enough your mother called me and said she'd work it."

"I wouldn't want her there alone," I said. "We've already had too much trouble—maybe more than the job's worth."

"Every job you want is worth whatever trouble there is to get it," he said solemnly. "Send Coulson and Annie with her. Coulson can watch things from the car." He nodded toward the door. Coulson stood down the hall, eyes wide and open, gun at ready. "I wouldn't worry about much with him around. I used to hunt with him when we was younger—back when you hunted for meat— not like them drunk, stubble-chinned deer slaughterers you get now. Coulson could shoot the eyes out of a blind woolly worm from fifty yards." He nodded, sure of his ground. "Anyone with sense won't bother around him."

"Go through the album once more," I said persuasively, nodding at it, unwilling to give it up.

He picked it up obligingly enough and went through it while I retreated to the kitchen, filled the ice bucket, and brought ice, Bourbon, and a pitcher of water back to the living room. Mom nodded at me from the sunroom when I went past it, then went back to her Gothic, content to be alone for now. She'd been a little subdued since the attack on the house.

Gosport was still looking through the album when I came back to the living room, but after a time he sighed and gave it up.

"There ain't nothing in there that means one solitary thing to me."

I fixed him a drink. He got rid of the tobacco and accepted it gratefully.

Annie came back to the door. She said: "Can I take the Monte over to the school libe? I need to look up a bunch of things."

"If you'll take Coulson with you," I said, nodding at the bailiff.

"I'd be most happy, young miss," Coulson called, over-hearing us.

Annie frowned. "Maybe I ought to take him at that. With all the police around here I doubt anyone's watching now, but with Mr. Coulson in tow at least my little deputy sheriff out there won't hound me for a date."

"You mean Joe Pierceton?" I asked, laughing. "It's your charm."

"Yes. He's persistent." She gave me a bright smile, scooped up the proffered keys, and led Coulson out the door. Outside I could hear them laughing and hooting at each other.

Later I called for Jen and brought her back for dinner. That was after Annie came back from the library. We watched television and I held hands with Jen and Mom insisted on her staying the night, which Jen did after only the lightest of protests. That made it possible for us to outwait the others.

You couldn't call it a complete nothing day.

Sunday you could.

Nothing.

11

To the Jury

On Monday morning I was in the courthouse quite early. I met a yawning Joe Pierceton coming from the office which once had been Ed's.

He eyed me in mock astonishment.

"You're up before the birds."

"Anything happened?" I asked, looking over the sleeping bag he carried idly over one shoulder.

"Nah. Maybe they know I'm waiting for them and are afraid of Lone Ranger Pierceton," he said, shrugging and grinning. "I'm going to quit in another day or so. This, and patrolling your house now and then, are ruining my night life."

"Quit anytime you want."

"I think maybe I'll stay one more night at least. Trial should be over by then and maybe things will calm down some."

"Thanks for all the help," I said. I went into my office and he disappeared down the hall. From my smudged window I witnessed him getting into a marked sheriff's car and zooming off a few moments later.

I read the instructions again.

Beyond the window the town came to life. Merchants opened stores, postmen passed briskly. I saw Half come up the sidewalk with his sidekick, Samdog, and watched them split a breakfast pint of wine. Politicians entered and exited the sheriff's office, getting their instructions from Amos, I supposed. Randy Rumple and a yawning Hen Zisk shook hands gravely below me without knowing I was watching. Zisk accepted a large, white envelope from Randy. Amos came idly out the door, smiling. He clapped them both on the back, looked up at my window, and said something. I did not think he could see me, as I was back away from the window. Whatever Amos said must have been funny. All laughed.

I sat and watched and had a moment of nostalgia for the days now past, the days when it had been all right, when there'd been no conflict, when I'd been another cog in the machine.

Through my door I could see the jurors arriving and that brought me back to present time. They passed my door and entered to wait in the jury room, ready to come out of it upon signal and take their places in the final act.

Higer came to my door. He was Monday-morning fresh, dressed in a deep blue suit and a wild tie. He looked like half a ton of money.

He said: "For the record, I'll want to renew my motion for a directed verdict, Judge."

"All right. When Jen gets here we'll have her show it."

He held out his hand. I took it and we shook vigorously.

"It's been a damned good trial," he said carefully. "My client keeps claiming to me that you're out to get him. I've told him I see no signs of it being that way." He shook his head wryly. "I'm not sure I'm getting through to him, but in my opinion, you've been most fair."

"Thanks."

He gave me a sidewise look. "And good luck to you in the election tomorrow. If my client has his way *there*, you're going to need it." With that warning, he nodded once more, and turned away.

Determinedly I went back to the instructions. Around me the noise continued to pick up.

The phone rang. Jen still hadn't arrived on the scene, so I answered it.

The voice was completely unfamiliar, muffled, far away, but not the one who'd called before.

The voice said: "Judge, you're going to dismiss the case against Amos. We've got your sister and your mother. You either dismiss or else." A pause, as if he'd lost his place on a printed statement. "Do you understand?"

"I hear you," I said. I listened carefully, trying to hear something in the background, but all I got was the click of the rehung phone.

I dialed home. Busy signal. I dialed again. The same. I began to worry more. I tried to be sensible. There were all those police around and reliable Coulson was there.

Jen came in as I sat there. I made my decision. I moved

up to her and whispered: "Don't say anything. Just let me have the keys to your car. I'm assuming you parked where you normally park."

Her eyes got huge. She gave me the keys and nodded.

"If I'm not back in twenty minutes have the local police and the state boys check the house." I patted her back reassuringly. "And hold it all together until then."

She nodded carefully, very much afraid.

I sprinted down the steps. Her car was in the side lot. Mine was parked in back where the sheriff could see it. I went out the side door and forced myself to walk casually to her car. It started at a touch of the key and I drove carefully out of the lot, hunched down a little in the seat and turned away from where I might be easily seen by a watcher at the sheriff's office.

Two blocks from the courthouse I recklessly increased speed.

I halted the car a block from home and parked it behind bushes. I cut through rain-dampened yards, startling at least one matron who was sipping coffee by her kitchen window.

The house looked normal. From my vantage point I couldn't tell if there were still police in front.

I went along the hedgerow and, after a time, gained the back porch.

The back door was locked and bolted. Through the edge of the curtain, seen dimly, I thought I could make out Coulson sitting at the kitchen table. As I strained to see him someone else came past down low. I thought it was Mom in her wheel chair. There was no sound.

I did hear something and, just for an instant, it sounded

like a scream. Then I smiled, recognizing the sound. It was Annie, singing in her fine soprano from upstairs.

I tapped carefully on the door. The curtain was pulled back and a rifle aimed at me. Coulson opened the door.

"Hey, it's you," he said amiably. Mom, who'd been out of sight, came back into the kitchen and rolled her chair up close and Annie followed her. I put my good arm on Annie's back and encircled her and put my artificial hand on the back of Mom's chair. I forced calmness into my voice.

"I got worried. Maybe the telephone line is down or something. I came home to check."

"There sure haven't been any calls," Coulson said.

"Not even for Anna," Mom joked.

I smiled and patted them both thankfully once more. I winked at Coulson, said good-by again, and drew him onto the back porch behind me. Mom puttered skillfully with Annie's breakfast.

"Be extra careful. Don't tell them, but there was another threatening telephone call and I think the phone wire here's been cut."

He nodded stolidly. He went back into the kitchen and I waited until he'd locked and bolted the door before I left.

———◆▶———

At eleven o'clock that night the jury tapped on the door and had the bailiff bring us news that they hadn't yet arrived at a verdict and that they'd like to rehear the instructions, break for the night, and come back in the morning.

We tracked down the lawyers and soon all were assembled again. Once more I droned the instructions, reading them slowly and carefully, balancing one for the state with one from the defense, while the jury listened gravely.

The bailiff took them out. The retired engineer and the schoolteacher walked close to each other, but not touching.

I went home and slept fitfully. Today had been May 1. Tomorrow, Primary Day, was May 2. Outside, the weather was still cold and unseasonable, but spring was upon us.

At three the next afternoon the jury tapped again on the door. We'd waited all day for them. I'd caught up on some paper work, tried a few default divorces, probated some wills, and even begun an attack on correspondence.

I'd voted and worked the polls for a little while at noon, while Mom and Annie had taken Coulson home for lunch.

An astute observer at the polls had told me a lot of people were voting, many more than usual. He didn't know what that meant.

Once again, when the message that a verdict had been reached came, I got everyone assembled. The defendant came over from the jail, this time in the loose custody of Sheriff Hen Zisk, who undoubtedly wanted to be in on the final act. Higer and Dunwich appeared. The clerk came up from two floors down.

"Ladies and gentlemen of the jury, have you reached a verdict?" I asked.

"We have," the semi-retired engineer said, standing. He held out a sheaf of papers, being all the prepared verdict forms we'd furnished the jury.

The bailiff brought them to the clerk. The clerk sorted them hastily, looking for the signed one. I watched his face, but could read nothing as he handed me the verdict to inspect. I read it silently and handed it back.

"Clerk will read the verdict," I ordered.

"We, the jury, find the defendant to be sixty-one years old and find that he is guilty of murder in the first degree and . . ."

First Degree. Life.

There were no cheers in the courtroom, and there was no outcry. A few reporters scrambled to get outside to call in the news, a few waited to talk to the participants.

At the defense table, standing with Higer, Amos bent just a little. He shook his head unbelievingly, but said nothing.

"Does the defendant desire to poll the jury?" I asked Higer.

"Defendant will waive polling the jury," Higer said, studying the unyielding faces in front of him, giving it up as a useless device.

I sat there on the high bench and watched prosecutor Allen Dunwich grinning and accepting congratulations from reporters and courtroom hangers-on. Once or twice he smiled at me.

And somehow, within me, I wondered if the show was over.

———————◄—◆—►————————

I stayed at the polls until six. Gosport McFay came past the house soon thereafter. Mom and Jen and Annie were nibbling at dinner and Gosport refused food or coffee. He led me away from the table.

"They really worked hard against you," he said. "They was even buying the courthouse-wall bums—your friends up there." He shook his head dolefully. "But a lot of people voted. A bunch. Biggest turnout we ever had in a primary I hear. The word about Amos getting convicted got out a little too late to help much." He smiled. "However, in some selected precincts, people were saying he'd been convicted even before it happened."

"You mean a false rumor was being spread?" I asked severely.

"You betchum."

"How unfair."

We grinned at each other.

"Old Amos. First degree. That's a real surprise." He shook his head. "And him with some guy on the jury who used to go with his niece."

"Who was that?"

"Some guy what used to be a engineer, but had a stroke or something. Kind of retired now. He's been going with Amos's niece—the one works in the auditor's office."

"Wait'll I tell Allen Dunwich *that*." And I wondered if a hung jury had been saved by the blossoming of a new romance.

Gosport soon left to go on to headquarters, but I decided that I'd not go there until all was decided and perhaps not go then. I kept thinking of the remaining pile of mail still stacked on my desk. I was a creature of habit and I'd become acclimated to being caught up, no matter how many hours that took. Besides, I was nervous from waiting. I left Coulson in charge and drove to the court-house. I had the radio on the local station, but reports were very sketchy and unofficial and the announcer kept predicting that it might be early morning before the results were known.

I entered and went down the broad central hall of the courthouse, skirting spittoons. Only the night lights were on in the hall. I waited for the elevator and it came creaking down to me, not inspiring much confidence with its sound, but better than walking up. As I ascended I could hear vague sounds from the second floor where the clerk kept his silent vigil awaiting official returns which everyone would see before he saw them.

I rode to my floor.

In my office the desk lamp made a single, small pool of light when I turned it on. I sorted through the rest of the mail, opening some and discarding it, making notes on pieces which needed answering. Then, after a time, I fell idle and stopped.

I sat there thinking.

A light shone dimly in the fog of my mind and then the fog cleared just a bit.

I suddenly had a very hazy idea of who had killed Ed Long. And if that were so, as I raced through it, it seemed to me that the same person might possibly have killed Janet Walker.

I dug through my desk and came out with a municipal phone directory for the city across the river. I found George Higer, Amos's attorney, listed therein. When the office number failed to answer I dialed his home, but no one answered there either. I remembered it was also primary election night across the river. He was probably involved in that.

I dialed Allen Dunwich's number. He answered after a time.

"Allen? I need to talk to you about Amos Walker's case. There might be a problem."

"Whatzit? Whoozis?" he asked. His voice was slurred, heavy with drink.

"I'll tell you in the morning," I said. "Come at nine o'clock."

"Allri—allri."

I grimaced, hung up, and thought some more. Up the street I could hear a little noise and I went to the window and looked out. A few people were beginning to gather on the lawn in front of the sheriff's residence. I didn't know why for sure. It could be to congratulate him. In the rear of the small crowd, guarded by Samdog Cabel and a couple of others, I saw Half in his cart. Whiskey would flow tonight. Free.

I picked up the phone to dial out again, thinking I'd check voting, but something had gone wrong. There was no answering buzz. I could walk down to the clerk's office downstairs.

I suddenly thought of something else, something I should have remembered long before. It was past time for me to be out of the courthouse.

I left my coat. I got up and ran for the door. It was too late. He awaited me there.

I never saw him, but I saw something. A cluster of stars smashed my head. I was moving away from them in old, combat remembrance when they hit me, and I was hit hard enough so that I went deep into a pool of dark water and was lost there.

For a long or short time it was like that.

12

Risk

When I came up and out it was very dreamy at first. My shirt had been removed and so had my pants, except for my shorts. I was cold. Somewhere outside I could still hear the primary night crowd. They were tearing it up, making a lot of noise. It came to me that Sheriff Hen Zisk must have won. I was sorry about that. If he'd won, then I'd undoubtedly lost. Logic.

A huge spot on my head beat scarily and painfully with each pulse of my heart. I felt all raw, inside and out. As I came more and more to awareness I hurt worse.

It was very dark where I lay. I could smell thick, moldy carpet. I had the impression of being inside a small area with walls all around me.

I tried moving. I was tied. My feet and my knees were tied and I also was tied at arm and shoulder level. My false arm and hand had been taken off. There wasn't much room to do anything. Panic rose within me and I fought it down.

I twisted and turned and tried to roll and was partially successful. One turn and I was up against something black and clinging which hung down from above me. I bunched the bottom of it against the wall behind me.

I knew where I was. Recognition was a thing of feel without sight, because there still was no light.

I was in the closet of my office, a large, walk-in type closet. The clinging thing above me was the robe I wore sometimes during trials. It seemed blacker than the darkness as I tried to see it.

I blinked my eyes some more, but there was nothing to see and blinking made my head hurt worse.

I considered the value of yelling and decided against it for the time being. I'd been in my office enough times at night working to know that no one was ever around—janitors long gone—no security. Two floors down there'd be a few people around the clerk's office, if it was still open and tabulating votes. I assumed it was because of the crowd noise outside. But between me and the clerk's office were two stories of stone and steel. I was insulated from them.

I heard footsteps from far away. I moved quickly back to what seemed to be the position I'd found myself in when I recovered consciousness. I closed my eyes and waited. Consciousness was a weapon I had against the unknown and I planned to protect it as long as I could.

The heavy closet door clicked open and whispered down its long, oiled hinges. A light shone on me and a booted foot prodded. I stayed limp and the boot came again, unsatisfied.

I heard the snap of a match lighting and steeled myself. In a moment I felt its heat searing my good hand. I fought and managed to keep my breathing normal. Somehow I kept from tensing away from the match.

Then the match was gone. The door closed again and I could hear the lock button click in.

I listened to footsteps move away. Somewhere, in the distance, I could hear some other noise. I tried to identify that noise. It came from Ed's office, but its sound meant nothing to me.

Before the visit to my dark closet by my assailant, before I'd been roughly examined to see if I was conscious, I'd had my one moment of panic, but I'd not had time to find the lump of fear that now grew within me. It had been as if I were only an onlooker watching something on television late at night. But the foot nudging and the match savagely applied had galvanized my sense of fear so that now that the blackness and aloneness were back I lay trembling and sweating on the dirty carpet.

I knew who was out there. I was surprised he'd known about my artificial arm. Maybe he'd found it when he removed my clothes. Surprise faded as I thought about the arm and my assailant. Although I'd kept the fact of loss hidden at the surface, what seemed hidden to me probably wasn't that way to anyone else.

I rolled over on my stomach and tested hard against the bonds. The ones that surrounded my arms and upper torso seemed to offer the best hope. A man who is bound is held because his hands are larger than his wrists and his wrists larger than the long bones above. Tying a man missing a hand is a difficult business. To combat that my attacker had tied me twice at arm level, once at wrist level on my good hand, then again at just above the elbows, pulling that one very tight, binding me cruelly. Then he'd looped the ropes above down to my feet and drawn them all together.

By pulling hard and shifting my body I found I could slide the bad arm out from underneath its elbow binding. That did little good, although it did give me breathing room. By experimentation I found that if I hunched up and pulled my feet toward me that gave me a little more slack within the ropes.

I remembered something. Up there above me, assuming he'd not seen it and removed it, my hook arm was hanging where I'd abandoned it. If I could get to it and get it on my stub, perhaps the hook could be used to help.

I rolled and bumped my way along on my back until I could feel myself against the correct wall. The carpet was a help as it muffled all sound.

Using my free arm stub, I managed to propel myself up enough to get my back against the wall. Doing that brought my head against the wall. For a time I thought it was all over and that I was going under again. Vision faded to white swirls. I was dizzy. I fought for and retained consciousness. I wondered just how badly I was hurt and what damage was done.

After a time I pulled my tightly bound legs back under me as far as I could and pushed up the wall. Up there, above me in the darkness, it seemed to me that I could almost see the hook hand. It was still above me, but I knew it couldn't be far. A few inches? A foot?

That distance might as well be ten miles. No matter how much I stretched and pulled and bumped and wriggled I couldn't reach the hand.

Another idea came. I tried to remember how I'd hung the hand. Not carefully, I hoped.

I bent over as far as I could and tried to jump. My feet would hardly leave the floor. Surely he must hear it outside.

I waited. No sound of approaching footsteps, no alarm yet.

I jumped twice—three times. At the last jump something struck my head a glancing blow and slid past me down my side. I felt the touch of sharp metal.

The hook hand.

I let myself slide back down to the floor, doing it carefully. Below me I could feel the hand. The harness arrangement was stiff from disuse, but I'd not need that part—at least at first.

The idea was to get my stub firmly lodged into the plastic sheath, then try to use the hook end as a tool to untie the rope around my good hand.

I wormed and squirmed and pushed. Twice I got the plastic over my stub, but had it slide off as I moved toward a wall to shove it on tight. The last time I was able to stay by the wall and work the hand on there.

Steps approached the closet, then stopped. We listened together. I could hear my own heart and breathing.

The steps receded. The noise outside had, if anything, increased.

I worked the hand back and forth. Pulling up was no good. It only loosened the shell. Trial and error.

The sweat ran down my nearly naked body despite the coolness.

I felt a rope I was pushing at give just a fraction. I worked the hook in there, pushing, pulling frantically, tearing the rope with the hook.

And then my good hand was out.

I raced through the rest of the bonds. In a few moments I stood shivering, completely unbound.

I put the hook arm on correctly. Then, because I was cold, I put on my judge's robe. It helped warm me a little.

I stood there for a moment and planned further moves.

I couldn't easily get out the closet door. It was locked from the outside and there was no way to open it from inside. There were oiled tracks that the doors ran on and I could, given time, remove the doors from those tracks, but he would hear me. If I was caught at it—and that seemed a sure thing, then I lost the value of whatever surprise was left to me.

Any lingering idea of trying that vanished as I heard footsteps come back into the room.

I thought for a moment he was coming for me, but he wasn't. I heard my little desk lamp click on and then the sound of someone riffling my papers. Probably checking to see if I'd made any notes, left any evidence.

I got back down on the floor quietly. The sound of my voice must come from low in the closet so he'd think I was still bound.

"Where am I?" I called quaveringly. "My head hurts."

All sound stopped except for the sounds of celebration coming from outside.

"I know you're out there," I said accusingly.

For a time I didn't think he'd say anything, but then he did: "Sorry about all this, Judge."

"Sure," I said. "I'm sorry, too."

"I can't figure out what they're doing out there," he said. "They've got a bonfire going and they threw something in it a few minutes back."

"You mean the crowd up in front of the sheriff's?"

He mumbled something. His voice wasn't quite right and I thought he was worried—not about me—about something going on that he couldn't figure.

"Maybe they're just celebrating Sheriff Hen's victory," I said. "Why not let me out of here?"

"Not yet, Judge." He laughed a little. "Soon though."

"Is this some kind of crazy joke?" I asked.

"You know better than that, Judge." I could almost visualize him smiling his good smile. "You've been busy trying your murder case, but not too busy to nose around way too much. I figured you might work things out. I figured it a long time ago, when you first got digging. Too bad for you, Judge. But it will all work out all right. Tonight you lose the election and are despondent. Damned windows in this place are hard to get open, but I've finally managed." He stopped for a moment and then went on accusingly: "You shouldn't have come back here. I knew you always did come back before to catch up after a trial. I took a chance you would again. Now, out the window."

"Maybe I didn't come alone."

"Oh yes. I watched you come in the door. If you'd figured it out before you'd have remembered something you gave me. And you'll lose the election by a lot of votes. We both realize that."

"Maybe," I said.

"You will," he said again, his voice confident.

"It all came clear a little while ago," I said.

"I heard you dial the phone from where I was listening. I was by the door. If you'd tried to say anything more than you did say I was going to just shoot you and take my chances. Fortunately for me, you didn't. Now, tomorrow, the prosecutor will just think it was some kind of deranged call made by a despondent man before suicide."

"If I figured it—others will."

"No." I could tell he wasn't sure.

"You did too many things poorly," I said. "The next person who really begins to think about it will find out what I was late in finding. I should have known much more quickly, because the whole thing was so very simple. You knew I was checking as soon as I started. Only a few people knew that. You had to find it out from one of them or from me. Then, when the drug business got to be part of it, I should have thought about something odd: We've never been able to get anyone to give us any drug information, even after conviction. You were in a position to keep them too frightened."

"A side benefit from the job," he admitted. "I just told them if they finked on me they'd never live to get out of the county jail. And they think I've got some people on the payroll up at state's prison. Maybe I have, maybe I haven't, but it's almost as good them thinking I have."

"Plus you needed a key to get in up here. You wanted to check over Ed's office and find out if he'd left anything behind. If Amos's people had wanted in all they'd have had to do was get a janitor's key. You couldn't get one that way so easily. So you scratched up the door and got your key from me on the pretense of watching things."

I heard a low chuckle of laughter.

I went on. "Whoever fired through my window and turned on my basement gas didn't really want to hurt me. I got a call to help alert me to the gas and you fired high through the window. I had to be here for the jury trial—I had to help remove Amos, if you got lucky enough. A bonus. Makes me wonder about something."

"Wonder away," he said. "There's a little time left."

"Could Amos be getting a big share of the area drug money? That would make it available elsewhere if he wasn't around."

"He isn't even involved. He got approached, but Amos don't like drugs."

"Then, why?"

"Because he was in the way. Get rid of Amos and maybe I move up the line. Sheriff Hen and Randy think they run things, but I imagine I could give them a battle for chairman, especially if they got to fighting among themselves—and I'd make sure they did. And besides, it wasn't supposed to happen this way."

"What you really mean is that if Amos didn't kill his wife then the police would still be looking for whoever did kill her?"

All that supposition brought was silence.

I started again: "Her situation helped me figure it out.

Here's this gal with nail scratches on her back. There's whiskey on the sink, the phone's been torn away. If you think about it long enough you can believe a love party gone bad rather than a husband-wife fight. Then there never was a weapon found. Who carries a weapon at all times and knows how to use it? Who can carry one without being suspect. You can, Joe. Someone said that Janet was going out with the sheriff. The thing is that anyone who drives a sheriff's car can and will be mistaken for the sheriff. Hen was and is too much in with Amos to be running his wife. He might chase any other wife, but not Amos's."

His voice was soft. "There's a lot of money in it, Judge. Them boys across the river pay real well. And if I need something done then they do it. Soon there'll be enough money for the rest of my life. I can be a somebody. There's just a few more loose ends to clear up. She was the first one. She was a tramp and she knew too much and wanted too much. She was going to divorce him and marry me. He'd have chewed me up and spit me out. I wouldn't have been a deputy no more. She wouldn't wait and give me time. She said she'd tell and someone might have believed her. She was pretty, but she was all tramp. I put on one of Amos's coats to keep me clean and I hit her with my stick. It felt good hitting her. I hit her a lot of times. Then when Ed went down and threw the stuff off the boat and cost me money I waited for him and hit him, too. I think he thought it was the sheriff's stuff at first, but it was my stuff. He came to me because I was passing information to you about politics and so I was a friend. I was one of your people. It was okay playing at that. If that guy from prison who was after you had come to town and I'd seen him I'd have shot him for you. Too bad he didn't come." His voice was almost wistful.

"Your boat?"

"In a way. It isn't in my name. It's just a bonus on things. Sheriff uses it more than me. He thinks it belongs to some folks across the river." He laughed a small laugh.

"That's another thing," I said. "You were the logical one for Ed to see at the sheriff's office. And I found out he did talk to you that first night."

"I saw him," he said. "Then, next night, he somehow knew. He came up through the yard and I was waiting for him out back, afraid he'd get to the sheriff before he got to me. He told me he'd dumped all that stuff in the river—God, lots of stuff—they didn't like that. They said I should have got him the night before. But I hit him and then I had the car to haul him away with. I hated to hit him with the car. I really did. Ed was okay to me."

"It's all done, Joe," I said. "Someone else will work it all out."

"No. I'll make me a lot more money and maybe I'll wind up being the top man around here. I ain't stupid like Zisk. He believes everything I tell him. I run his office. He can't hardly read or write. I smile and folks like me." He stopped for a moment. "You know who I really want to like me now?"

"No," I said, although I'd guessed.

"Your sister. I'd sure like that."

"She thinks you're a bug," I said.

I could tell that made him a little angry, which was what I wanted.

He tried to dig into it a little further. "I'll wait around and not push. She's awful young. She'll remember I watched the house. She'll remember I was your friend. And maybe . . . soon . . ."

"I told her I didn't like you, Joe," I lied. "You're a bug to her."

I heard him shifting out of the chair and moving toward the door. I came up quickly and silently. He fumbled with the lock, then shoved the door open, ready to reach down for me, night stick in hand.

I'd spread my arms and I came out of the closet for him in my robe like a black devil, hook arm up and slashing at his eyes.

He screamed like a woman and fell back. Down the hall it seemed to me that I heard something else, a new sound.

He swung at me with the night stick with a swift, snakelike move. I caught the club on my hook and hit him very hard with my right hand. It was shoulder high, but it rocked him some. He hit at the hook arm again and this time he caught bone, but I fought off the pain and kept the hook in front of his face.

In his eyes I saw the realization dawn that he might lose and he went for his belt and the gun that was holstered there. I smacked at the hand that reached with my hook and caught him very flush with a right hand to the face. It smashed his nose and I felt bone go.

He screamed again and quit trying for the gun. He fell away from me and covered his face. I let him cover up. I reached down and took the club and gun from his hands.

I thought maybe my arm was broken inside the plastic sheath. It hurt a lot.

Outside, in the corridor, the noise was now tumultuous. There was a crowd out there in the hall.

I opened the door. Gosport peered over my shoulder and saw Joe Pierceton, his tan uniform spotted with blood. Half was there, with Samdog.

Gosport said dubiously: "You won."

———◆———

I had several other moments that were worth while. One was sitting on the bench with my bad arm in a sling and granting Amos a new trial. It didn't make a lot of difference to him. He still hated my guts. I thought he'd arranged for someone to call me on the last day of the trial, but I couldn't prove it.

Another was childishly not shaking hands with Randy Rumple, who was suddenly willing to let bygones be bygones. I supposed I was, too, but I just didn't want to shake hands.

Then there was listening to Half tell me how he'd organized the courthouse bums, accepted the proffered cash, then had his crew vote for me—even Samdog Cabel (if he hadn't forgotten).

My margin was five hundred plus votes, too many for a recount, too many to try stealing it.

I also heard about how the mob outside had burned Hen Zisk in effigy after it became apparent he was beaten—after only a few precincts were in, and long before I was assured of winning. That had been the commotion outside the courthouse.

Joe Pierceton, in jail, was trading names across the H

river as he plea bargained for his life. Ed's appointment book and some things police theorized were from Ed's wallet had been found in Joe's room. Police had also found an envelope with my name on it. All it contained was a note from Ed to me about a runaway child. Sometime later, looking, I never could find a photo with Joe Pierceton in it in Ed's album or on his wall.

The best was going with Jen (without Mom) and getting house plans to look over. We decided to build back in the shade, right where the trees were tallest, where there's just room for a cottage.

Somehow all of this had put things back into proper perspective for me. If I'd not lost the arm, then maybe I'd have lost my life. Something to think about. Mom reminded me of it twice just yesterday.